What readers are saying about
Miracle's Destiny:

"A Great Family Story!" ~S. Cox

"Captivating Characters!" ~C. Holloway

"I enjoyed the book and it kept my interest." ~An avid reader, MD

"Five Stars!" ~A male reader in Texas

"A Best Seller!" ~Libby C.

Also by Georgette Littlejohn

Children's Book

A GRO-c-ERY STORY

MIRACLE'S DESTINY

Georgette Littlejohn

Published by Philadelphia Publishing House
Philadelphia Publishing House
938 E. Swan Creek Road, Suite 412
Fort Washington, Maryland 20744

PHILADELPHIA PUBLISHING HOUSE

This book was published by Philadelphia Publishing House for the sole purpose of entertainment.

This book is a work of fiction. All names, characters, incidents and places are fictitious.

ADULT READING MATERIAL

Cover design: Patrise Henkel

Editing: Cheryl Robinson

Print Formatting: By Your Side Self-Publishing
www.ByYourSideSelfPub.com

To contact Author Georgette Littlejohn, or to be placed on a mailing list to receive information about new releases and updates, email the author at: authorgeorgettelittlejohn@gmail.com. You may also follow the author's blog at: www.geelovestowrite.wordpress.com.

DEDICATION

This book is dedicated to my husband. Thank you for always believing in me and supporting me through my many adventures.

You've never stifled my visions or dreams no matter how crazy or absurd they may seem. I look forward to growing old with you!

ACKNOWLEDGMENTS

First, I must give honor to God.

Words can't express how grateful I am that his grace and mercy is new every day. He continues to bless me even when I don't deserve it!

I would be remiss if I didn't acknowledge several people. Anyone who says they can make it alone with no help is someone I would run from… we ALL NEED HELP.

To Madison and Justina… my cheering section who encourage me when I want to quit and think I don't have what it takes to put the words on the paper I extend a heartfelt thank you!

To Cheryl, my writing mentor, if not for you I would still be a writer and not an author. The extra push and constant demands helped me reach my next level. Please continue to pay-it-forward to other authors. You will receive your reward from the Master so don't measure your rewards based on what man does-you will be disappointed.

Finally, to my family and friends that have supported me in all I do… I say thank you and I love you all.

Chapter One

Miracle

"Oh Shit! Oh Shit! Oh Shit! Yes, yes, yes. That's it baby… that's it. I'm cumming. I'm cum…"

The phone rang right at the exact moment Mychal was going to release all his manly juices into Miracle's moist and ripened vagina. It had been two weeks since the two had time to become intimate and they both were raving like wild animals in the jungle. They never had any issues when it came to the bedroom. One thing was for sure, sex, love making, screwing or whatever term they decided to use this week, it was never a problem. Often, Miracle and Mychal would not speak for days, but they would come together and cohabitate magically and go right back to not speaking for several more days. It's amazing and crazy, at the same time—when the bodies are connected sexually, nothing else matters.

"Please, baby, don't answer that right now," Mychal pleaded in a low raspy voice.

His manhood was harder than Fort Knox. He was backed up like the Brooklyn Bridge in rush hour traffic and he wanted to release it, now.

"Are you fucking kidding me? Some one better be dead.

Who the hell is calling at this damn hour anyway?" Mychal snapped again.

"Maybe, they will hang up," Miracle whispered.

Shit, Miracle thought, she needed this just as much as he did. Unfortunately, she hadn't cum, yet; but it was still good. Mychal knew how to make her body scream. He knew every curve and inch of her body. He knew where to stroke, when to touch and how to move. It always took her longer to reach her climax, but she would get there. Who in the hell was calling at this hour?

The phone kept ringing and ringing.

"Mychal, I have to answer it. It's going wake up the entire house, if I don't."

"Goddammit! Somebody better be dead!"

"Mychal!" Miracle yelled and rolled over to pick up the phone. "Hello," Miracle said, but couldn't understand the caller.

"Who is this? Calm down. What are you saying? I can't understand you. Please, you are scaring me," Miracle mumbled.

"Joey, is that you? Joey, Joey, I need you to calm down. I can't understand you, baby. What are you saying?" Miracle begged.

"Oh, no!" Miracle covered her mouth, when she finally comprehended what he was saying.

"Joey, I'm so sorry. It's going to be okay," Miracle continued, as she tried to hear Joey through his sobbing.

"Who is there with you? Where are you? Joey, please, baby, calm down. Let me speak with Mark. I know. I know. Put Mark on the phone," Miracle pleaded with Joey.

Joey finally handed the phone to Mark.

"Hello, Mark. He is a mess. Is there any way you can give him something to calm him down? What happened?" Miracle inquired.

"Okay, I understand. I know Joseph should be the one to tell me, but he is a wreck right now and I can't get anything out of him. Mark will you please stay with him until I get there? I will try to get a flight out later today. Thanks, Mark, I really appreciate it."

Joseph was screaming hysterically in the background.

"Mark, can you please put him back on the phone," Miracle broke in. "Oh, God!" Miracle sighed.

"I will try, Mark replied. He is running around the room screaming at the top of his lungs. Joseph, Joseph, please, come get the phone and talk to Miracle," Mark requested in a stern, but soft voice.

Joseph grabbed the phone. "Dead! Miracle. Tracey's dead! Jesus, dead!"

"Joey, Joey, listen to me, baby. I will be there. I am going to get a flight out later today and be there soon. Joey you must pull yourself together. I don't know what is going on, but I will be there soon."

Miracle caught her breath.

"I love you, Joey. Please, try to get some rest and I'll see you soon." Miracle hung up the phone.

Mychal was staring at her.

"What the hell was that all about?" Mychal spat.

He was still upset lying there in his birthday suit that the good Lord generously blessed him with. Mychal was 6'5" lean, but very muscular and the color of hot tar. He was so black that he shined. He had played basketball since he could walk straight and he always had an athlete's body. His skin was silky smooth and he took great pride in making sure it was always well moisturized. He was so dark that he never wanted to be called ashy.

Mychal knew kids were cruel, so he made sure that he took care of his skin. It didn't fail him either. It also helped that he was a talented basketball player. He knew he had to do something to stand out. He never wanted to be teased and he knew with skin that color he would be, so he picked up a talent and mastered it. Instead of people teasing him, they wanted to be him. The things he could do with a basketball, others only dreamed about. He was sure to be the next big thing.

"It was Joseph," Miracle responded. "I don't know what is going on. He just kept screaming dead. I'm going to have to get a flight down there, later today."

"Who is he talking about?"

"I don't know," Miracle lied.

She knew exactly who he was talking about, but she lied because she wasn't ready to open that can of worms, right now. Mychal was already pissed because he was interrupted in the middle of reaching Mt. Rushmore. This was not the time to have this conversation with him. She hated lying to her husband, but this was for the best if she intended on getting any sleep. She had a long day ahead and from the looks of things, it was going to be a doozy.

Mychal gave Miracle a skeptical look and shrugged his shoulders. His mind was on one thing—his hard penis.

"Oh, well… since you're leaving later today, we might as well finish what we started before the damn phone rings again," he grinned.

He rolled on top of Miracle and began kissing her body from head to toe. Her body tingled and some tension was released. She still had Joey on her mind, but right now, she needed this more than anything.

She could only imagine what she was walking into. It was no telling with Joey. She let her mind wander back to when she met Mychal and how they used to have sex any and everywhere. Her thoughts took her back to one evening, when they were on Mychal's apartment balcony and he sat her down in a chair. He slowly removed her shorts and panties, opened her legs and started licking on her toes through her thong sandals. He made his way up to her toned legs and landed at the women's most precious spot! The memory made Miracle let out a low moan that excited Mychal and urged him to finish the task expeditiously. Damn, she loved this man. Even after all of these years, he still had it. He landed his mouth on that spot again and Miracle was in euphoria.

Chapter Two

Miracle

The alarm clock screeched and Miracle sat straight up in the bed. She really hated the alarm clock and had been saying for years that she was going to trash it, but never had. She had it since college and now could not bring herself to throw it away. Her mom gave it to her when she left home, because she was so worried the girl would never make it to class on time.

She remembered her mom saying. "Baby, you know you're a hard sleeper. Take this clock. I know it's loud, but you won't miss class," her mother explained. She was so proud of Miracle.

"Thanks, mom." She didn't know she would go deaf in the process of not missing class.

Miracle smiled at the memory as she hit the snooze button on the damn annoying alarm.

"Five more minutes, please." Just five more she pleaded with herself. She reached next to her, but she already knew that Mychal was out of the bed. He rose without the call of an alarm. He was probably on mile four or five by now, and making his way back home. She fell back on the pillow and grabbed her forehead. She thought of Joey and what the hell was going on with him. She would call him a little later, after she had her flight information. She had to get the kids out of the house first and make sure dad was okay.

"Dad!" *Oh, hell, what was she going to do with Dad? Just relax Miracle. Five more damn minutes.* She thought as she closed her eyes.

"Good morning, Dad," Miracle greeted him and smiled, as she walked into the kitchen.

"Morning, baby," Patrick responded.

The kids were sitting around the table eating breakfast and Patrick was reading the paper. That was one good thing about having her dad there. He was a cook in the Marines in his early days and when he retired, he was a Chef for the government, until he retired, again. He always made sure the kids had breakfast in the morning, if she slept late.

"Thanks, Dad!"

"No problem, baby girl. You know I'll do anything for my baby." He smiled.

Her dad was still as handsome as he could be to her. His hair was turning salt and pepper, as well as, his beard. He reminded her of Richard Roundtree, except he's more handsome, of course. People used to always stop us when we were out asking for his autograph, because they thought he was the famous actor.

My dad would just smile and say, "No, no you're making a mistake. I'm not him."

I'm sure it boosted his ego a bit. My mom would just grab his arm a little tighter and pull him even closer.

"Mom, don't forget I have practice tonight. Are you or dad picking me up?"

Mason asked.

"Huh?" Miracle was still miles away.

"I have basketball practice tonight. Who's picking me up?" Mason repeated.

"Probably, your dad."

"Dad, what?" Mychal interjected as he walked in with sweat dripping from everywhere.

"I have to go out of town," Miracle responded ignoring Mychal.

"What? Why?" Mason inquisitively asked.

"Out of town," Patrick chimed in. "What's going on?"

Mychal shot Miracle a look like yeah what's going on. She rolled her eyes at him. She hated when he was being a smart ass in front of the kids.

"Is everything okay, baby girl?" Patrick inquired. Miracle really didn't want to get into it right now.

"Yeah, is everything okay, Miracle?" Mychal shot at her.

She could have thrown the coffee cup she had in her hand right at his head. Mychal just smiled.

He is such an ass sometimes, Miracle thought to herself. Of course, all eyes were on her. McKenzie was staring also. Usually, she could count on her daughter to have her back, but this time she was out there all by herself.

"Uhm, Uhm… I have to go to Atlanta to check on Uncle Joey. I'm not sure what's going on, I can't really say right now, but I just know that I have to go down there. I will only be gone for a couple of days. Dad should be able to handle things here, while I'm away," she said sarcastically.

She licked out her tongue at him playfully. She knew that was a joke. She would call Rosita, her backup housekeeper, to see if she was available to help out while she was in Atlanta. Miracle remembered when she went away on a girl's weekend getaway a few months ago and all hell broke loose. Mychal claimed he could handle the kids.

Yeah right. He fell apart.

She got back to the house being a damn disaster—the kids had pretty much missed every routine weekend activity and had run buck wild for two days. The image was permanently burned in her mind.

"Oh, hell, no!" Miracle said out loud. Rosita would be called and she prayed she was available.

One more damn thing to do on her never-ending list.

"Geez! Mom, who's going take me to dance class?" McKenzie finally spoke up.

"I can take you, pumpkin," Mychal replied.

"Mom," McKenzie retorted looking at her mom.

"Don't worry, baby. You will get there. I got everything

under control. Always do."

"Really?" Mychal crooned as he walked passed and tapped her butt.

Mychal added, "I'm going to take a shower, since you have everything under control."

"Yeah, do that, you stink."

How can you love and hate someone so much at the same time? she wondered.

"Get finished, guys. The bus will be here soon. I can't afford for y'all to miss the bus, today. Not today. If I'm not here when you get home from school, I will call later and check in on you guys."

Mason and McKenzie finished their breakfast and gathered their things to leave.

"What no hugs and kisses," Miracle called out.

Mason gave his mom a look that said, "I'm too old for that!"

"Boy, get your butt over here. I bet you don't have a problem kissing up on those little fresh girls at school."

"Really, mom!"

"Yeah, really!"

Mason hugged his mom and kissed her on the cheek. "Later!" he breathed.

"Later!" she retorted.

McKenzie grabbed her and hugged her tight.

"See you, mom. Have a safe trip. Love you!"

"Love you too, baby." Miracle smiled as she watched her children walk out of the kitchen. Those were her babies. She didn't care how old they got, they would always be her babies.

"Okay, baby girl, the kids are gone. What the hell is going on with that brother of yours, now?"

"Dad, I really don't know," Miracle lied again.

Mychal hadn't left for work—yet; and she didn't want to take the chance of him walking in on their conversation. Miracle hated when her dad grilled her. She felt like she was a kid all over again. He had a way of making her feel like an innocent child and not a grown-ass woman.

"He called a little after midnight, crying, screaming and

repeating the word dead. I have no clue what the heck is going on with Joey. I tried talking to him on the phone, but that wasn't working. He wouldn't give me anything. Mark was there, but he wouldn't tell me what was going on either. He said that I would have to hear it from Joey, so that's why I am headed down there today, to find out what's going on."

"That boy is always in some shit," Patrick spat.

"I remember when he was in high school and we got a call at two am in the morning from the police, asking if we knew where our son was. And of course, I said that he's in his damn bed."

"Sir, I think you should go check," the policeman said.

I did and he wasn't there.

The policeman said, "I believe, we have your son, here. He was just picked up with a group of kids, who stole a car. They hit a tree, then, the car went into the pool in someone's backyard."

"He was with that damn Mark," Patrick spat.

"Every time he was with Mark, he got in trouble. I hated him then, and I hate him now."

"Dad it wasn't Mark. It was Matthew. He just met Mark when he moved to Atlanta."

"It was Mark. Don't tell me. I know who it was," Patrick adamantly stated.

"Mark. I remember it, just like it was yesterday. I was the one who got the call, not you."

Miracle just took a deep breath and grabbed her forehead. She did not feel like this right now. She did not want to get into a pissing match with her dad over Joey right now. This was the one subject that could definitely trigger whatever his condition was and she just was not in the mood for it. She had too much to do.

"Okay, dad, you're right. Mark."

"I know I'm right." He mumbled under his breath.

Miracle kissed him on the cheek and walked out of the kitchen, leaving him mumbling and looking at the newspaper.

Miracle entered the library and turned on the computer. She figured she would get her business taken care of instead of arguing with her father about Joey. She managed to get everything done. When she emerged from the library, it was early afternoon. She had booked a flight for later in the evening. She needed to pack and make sure everything was together for Rosita when she arrived. She was relieved that she could reach Rosita and she was available to come and stay with the family. Miracle was headed upstairs and passed by the family room where she saw her father sitting on the couch watching Family Feud with Steve Harvey.

"Sex," he screamed.

"Dad! What in the world?" Miracle exclaimed.

"Family Feud." He grinned.

"They asked 100 men, 'what's the number one thing wives hold back from their husbands'."

"Really, dad?"

"Yup!"

"I'm going to pack," Miracle smirked.

"It's true, baby girl. Sad, but true. Did you find out what's going on with Joseph?"

Patrick questioned.

"No, not yet. I was going to call him, when I got upstairs. I have a flight out later this evening."

"Okay. I'll be here waiting." He turned his attention back to the television. Miracle shook her head and walked out of the room.

"Hello, Joey." She paused, while he responded.

"Joey you don't sound good. What's going on?"

His voice sounded as if he were slurring his words.

"What have you taken, Joey? I can barely understand you. You're scaring me."

Miracle continued, "I have a flight out in a couple of hours. I will be there soon. Joey, can you, please, tell me what is going on?"

Miracle listened to Joey once more.

"What? What are you saying? Joey? Joey?"

The thud of the phone hitting the floor was the only response Miracle received.

"Hello? Hello?"

"Hey, Miracle. It's Mark. He's kind of heavily sedated, right now. It was the only way we could get him to calm down."

Miracle was hanging on to Mark's words.

"He wouldn't stop screaming and running around the house. I called the doctor over earlier and he gave him some medication to calm him down. He was in shock. I didn't want to do it, but, baby, I had no choice. He was acting like a madman. None of your family is here, so I had to make the decision. I hope you're not mad at me."

"No, not at all, Mark. I understand. However, can you, please, just tell me what is happening? It's obvious, I can't get any information from Joey, so you are the next best thing."

"Uhm, I really didn't want to do this over the phone. "I know you are worried out of your mind."

"I just want to know what happened," Miracle pleaded.

"I know you do, but you should have that conversation with Joseph," Mark insisted.

"You're right, you're right. I'm sorry, Mark." She paused and added, "I'm just shocked that's all. I will see you guys shortly. I was about to pack. I'll be there soon."

Miracle sighed. "Give him a big hug and kiss for me, please."

"I will. Just get here. He needs you," Mark said as he hung up the phone.

Miracle began weeping. Hot tears rolled down her cheeks. She sat frozen for a few minutes trying to take it all in. She couldn't imagine what Joseph was going through. The worst part was that she couldn't even share the news with Mychal. Not just yet. Miracle had to get to Atlanta first and check on Joey.

Damn, why now? She got up and began packing.

Chapter Three

Joseph

Joseph was in a tranquilized state. He was gone. His body was there, but his mind was many miles away. He was remembering his wedding day.

It was perfect from beginning to end. People say that there is no perfect wedding day. Well, not true. Their day was PERFECT! It was just as they had envisioned it. He couldn't believe that it had only been six months. It was way too soon. This just wasn't fair.

Who the hell loses their spouse after only six months of marriage? God had to be playing some kind of cruel joke. Maybe, he was being pranked.

Mark was always playing jokes on him. This had to be one of his elaborate jokes. But he went too far this time. Joseph tried to scream at Mark to stop the joking and bring Tracey back, but nothing would exit from his vocal cords. It was like they were ripped from his throat. His whole body was numb. Every fiber of his being was stiff. He felt like he was dead himself. It was like rigor mortis had set in. If this wasn't death, it might as well be.

How would he survive? Tracey was gone. His life. His love. His very existence.

He wanted to cry but his ducts were dehydrated. They could produce nothing—not one single teardrop.

"Joseph, why don't you go and try to lie down. You really need to go get some sleep. You have been awake for 24 hours now. This is not healthy. You're starting to scare me," Mark uttered.

"Did you hear what the doctor said? If you don't get some rest soon, he is going to come back and give you something to make you sleep for a couple of days or take you to the hospital and make you stay there until you rest," Mark added.

"Please, at least just go lie down and rest your body. It will help," Mark pleaded again.

Joseph was thinking, *Help. Nothing will fucking help other than Tracey being risen from the dead like Lazarus. If Tracey doesn't walk through that door right now, then nothing will help.*

"Nothing!" Joseph finally managed to scream.

"Joseph, please calm down. I just want you to try to get some sleep. You look awful. If you only knew how you looked, you would be running to the bed," Mark smiled. He tried to lighten it up.

Joseph had always been big on his looks. He never left the house unless he was put together from head to toe, no matter what the task or event.

Mark whispered in a low voice, "Joey, I can't imagine what you're feeling, but you must rest. You will be no good to yourself or anyone for that matter, if you don't get some rest. People will start arriving soon and at some point you are going to have to start making arrangements. You will not be able to think clearly and do the wonderful things you do with no rest."

Mark waited for Joey to answer him and when he didn't, he continued, "I know you, and you are only going to want the best for Tracey. You would not be able to live with yourself, if it is something less. It would be what Tracey would want as well."

Somehow that seemed to soften Joseph. Mark had a way of playing with Joseph's psyche. He had to turn it around and make it all about his skills and what he could do.

The notable Joseph Jones could not put on an event without it being talked about, even if it was a funeral. Atlanta always had his events on their lips. Joseph was the events extraordinaire of ATL. People sought him out to handle their events. His events were like magic in the making.

"I guess, I should go lie down," Joseph sighed at Mark.

"Yes, you should. You will feel better and look better," Mark shot back.

Then, replied, "No, seriously, Joey, I'm sure you will feel better once you get some rest. Hopefully, by the time you wake up, Miracle will be here, and you all can begin to make arrangements."

"Thanks, Mark, I really appreciate you being here." Joseph managed to get the words out. "I know, I've been a hot damn mess and you've put up with my craziness. It means a lot to me. I know it will probably get worse, before it gets better, so please just bear with me. However, I lost my best friend, my love, my life. It's going to take me some time."

"Of course," Mark responded. "I wouldn't dare think it would be any other way. Joseph, I will be here for as long as you need me. I'm your friend."

He thought a moment and said, "When you hurt, I hurt. I loved Tracey, as well. This is difficult for me, too. I'm being strong for you, but trust me, it's not easy. Take all the time you need, my friend. That is part of the healing and grieving process. We all experience it, just in different ways. However, we must remember… time is the healer of all wounds. But each person's time is personal. Now, go lay down!"

Miracle descended the stairs with her suitcase and carry-on bag. Her dad was still watching television.

"Dad, you still in front of the television?"

"Sure am, baby girl. I ain't bothering nobody, so don't bother me."

"I'm about to head out to the airport."

"You're leaving before the kids and Mychal get home?"

"Yes. This was the only flight going to Atlanta, and I need to get there today. I got in touch with Rosita. She is going to get the kids from school and take them to their activities. She will be here the next couple of days until I return. Treat her nice. Dad, please, don't say any inappropriate comments."

"Who, me?" Patrick stated shyly.

The last time Rosita was there she almost quit by the time Miracle had returned. Her dad had said some pretty off the wall stuff. Miracle knew her dad was going through something, but that wasn't even it. Patrick was just being an asshole—plain and simple.

"Well, did you call Joey? What is so pressing that you must be in Atlanta today?"

Patrick smirked.

"It's Tracey."

"Apparently, Tracey died last night."

"Died. What the hell you mean died? What happened?"

"I don't know, dad. I'm just as shocked as you are. Joey couldn't even explain. He is a wreck. Once I get all the details, when I get there, I will be able to shed some light on the whole situation."

"Okay, baby girl, I'm going to take your word for it. I will leave it alone until you get there, but you can bet your ass in grass that I will be waiting for you to call back here."

Huh! Here we go again, Miracle thought to herself.

The doorbell rang right on queue and saved her from her dad's shenanigans. Miracle walked to the door. She already knew it was the car service. She wasn't expecting anyone else. The driver grabbed her bags and walked them out to the black Lincoln Town car and placed them in the trunk.

"Give me a few minutes, please, and I'll be right out.

"Absolutely, Ma'am." He nodded his head and got into the driver's seat and closed the door.

Miracle walked over to the cream and black marble top accent foyer table and picked up her purse. She dug inside and pulled out an envelope addressed to Mychal. She sat it on the table.

Miracle gave her dad a hug and kissed his cheek. "I'll call you guys when I get there. Remember, dad, be good," she called out as she exited the house. She was a little nervous about leaving her dad at home alone, but Mychal would be there in less than an hour and she had nosey Ms. Lawson from across the street watching the house. She had been alerted to call immediately, if anything looked suspicious. Miracle knew Ms. Lawson had no problem doing just that. She was their private neighborhood watch.

Chapter Four

Miracle

Miracle took a quick moment to compose herself, before ringing the doorbell. She knew Joey was going to be a mess and she had to be strong. Everyone knew they could depend on her to always be the strong one.

Get yourself together Miracle. Now, isn't the time. It's not about you, girlfriend.

Miracle rang the bell and Mark answered the door.

"Miracle!" he exclaimed grabbing her and giving her a big hug.

"I'm so glad you're here." He looked her over and hugged her again. "You're looking good, girl. Did you lose some weight?"

"I don't think so," Miracle chuckled.

She was in one of her good weight places, right now. Her 5'7" body was carrying her 165 pounds well. Her skin resembled a freshly baked golden brown pound cake. Yo-yos should have been her favorite toy, because that's what her weight did… yo-yo. She had tried pretty much every fad diet there was, but couldn't stick with it more than a week.

Mark kissed her cheek. "Well you look great!"

"Mark, please, you're always trying to make a girl feel good."

"Let me take your bags."

Mark reached for her suitcase and carry-on bag from her shoulder. Miracle closed the door and followed Mark into the condo. The place was immaculate, as always. Joseph had been a neat freak, since he was a child. Miracle was amazed, even as kids, he always had everything in order. All of his toys were color coordinated and his closet was neat and organized.

He used to always come to her room and shake his head and say, "Miracle, this room is a disaster."

"I know where everything is. Whatever I need is right at arm's length," She would joke.

"Yeah that's the problem. Everything is at arm's length," Joey would retaliate.

Miracle smiled at the memory. They had a lot of good memories from their childhood, but their family was not without issues. All families had some type of dysfunction; it just would depend on the family as to how severe.

Bring it back, Miracle. Now is not the time to hash up old memories.

"Where is Joseph?" She had to get back to the present.

"He's lying down," Mark replied. "I finally got him to take a nap. He had been up for 24 hours straight and was a hot mess. He was literally running around the house screaming and yelling. Hmmm… Let's get some tea and talk."

Mark sat Miracle's bags down next to a 1940's mahogany breakfast table that was decorated with little knickknacks from Joey's travels. There was a wedding picture of Joey and Tracey in the middle of the table. Miracle paused for a moment to look at the picture. They looked so happy in the picture. They were smiling and had their whole lives ahead of them.

What the hell happened? She thought. *That was only six months ago.*

"I know," Mark broke her gaze. He knew what she was thinking, as well.

They walked down the hall and into the kitchen. Miracle could never decide if the kitchen, Joseph's room or hell, the bathroom was the best room in the house. The whole damn house was just super chic stylish. Joey had the eye. That was his gift and thank goodness, he knew it and so did everyone else. He had been styling, as long as she could remember. Joey would sit for hours drawing and styling whatever he got his hands on.

Their father would get so upset. "What are you doing, boy?" He would yell.

"Boys don't do that."

"Miriam, what the hell is wrong with this boy?" he'd ask.

My mom would look my dad straight in the eye and say nothing. Miriam didn't play. She took a lot from my dad, but when it came to her children—that was one area she didn't budge. You couldn't talk about her babies—nobody! That meant NOBODY. She was the sweetest women you ever wanted to meet and would give you the clothes off her back and her last dime, but talk about her children and another side appeared. It was scary. That was the Miriam you didn't want to meet.

The sound of the cabinet closing bought Miracle back to the kitchen.

"What kind of tea do you want, Miracle? Girl, you were a million miles away,"

Mark chuckled.

"Sorry. This just has me thinking of things from the past. I guess death does that. Bring up forgotten memories that were buried. I'll take Peppermint tea."

Mark went over to the oversized panty and pulled out Joseph's plethora of gourmet teas. The commercial gas range had 10 burners. *Who needed 10 burners?*

The Alessi bird whistle tea kettle was atop the first burner. Mark was moving around the kitchen like it was his own space.

He and Joseph and been friends for over 10 years, since Joseph moved back to the states. He felt really comfortable in the space. That's how Joey made you feel, once he accepted you into his world. You had to be accepted. If not, it could get pretty ugly.

"Sugar or honey?" Mark asked.

"Honey. Does he have any fresh lemons or lemon juice?"

she replied.

"Of course," Mark responded.

Miracle took a seat at the large center island that sat six. The high back leather swivel chair was chartreuse. The kitchen walls were a light gray. The upper cabinets were white and the lower cabinets were the color of steel wool. There were accents of chartreuse and orange sprinkled around the kitchen.

There was a feature wall on the far side of the kitchen that had a one-of-a-kind piece of artwork painted by one of Joseph's friends—just for him. It was a scene from Italy, when Joey had traveled there. He had stopped for dinner one night at this café, when the sun was setting and the weather was perfect. He said that love was in the air. The setting was great, the food was exceptional and it was one of the best moments of his life, so he wanted to always remember it. He described it to his friend and the artist recreated what he thought Joey saw and painted it, especially, for his kitchen wall. Joey loved it. It was beautiful. The colors were so vivid. The painting just drew you in when you looked at it—a breathtaking scene. She noticed something different every time she looked at it. Then, Miracle turned her attention back to Mark.

"So, tell me what in the world has Joey been doing? You mentioned, he has been screaming and yelling around here like a crazy person."

"Child, yes," Mark laughed. "Girl, I thought I was going to have to commit him, seriously. I was so glad to see Dr. Watson. I was getting scared, Mir."

"I bet," Miracle sighed as she stirred her tea.

"He went from screaming and yelling to silence. He wasn't even blinking. He was just sitting there staring into space for hours. When he didn't move to go to the bathroom, I knew it was time to call the doctor."

"Wow," Miracle murmured.

"It was getting serious. It's definitely an issue, when you don't move to go to the bathroom."

"Damn straight," Miracle replied. "I'm just glad you were here. No telling what would have happened, if you hadn't been here with him."

"Depression is real. It can make you do things you hadn't even imagined before."

"I can't thank you enough," and Miracle grabbed Mark's hand. Then, she added, "You always come through in the clutch for Joey. He is blessed to have such a friend like you. As a matter of fact, I don't think he considers you a friend any more. I know he calls you his brother. You truly mean a lot to him."

"Who means a lot to who?" Joseph interrupted. "I know you're not telling him he means a lot to me," Joseph smiled wryly.

"I see a nap has perked someone up. Glad you feel better," Mark joked.

"Mir, I'm so glad you're here."

Miracle stood up and they met each other in the center of the kitchen and embraced for several minutes. Miracle could feel Joey's heart beating. It was beating so fast. She embraced him tighter.

"Joey, yes, I'm here."

Joey was trying so hard, not to break down in her arms. His sister was always his safe haven. She was the only one in his family who was ever there for him. No one else understood him. But she got it. She never judged. She never questioned. She loved Joseph for Joseph.

"Come get some tea," Mark interjected.

They walked over hand-in-hand. Miracle was looking at Joey. He looked like he had aged, since she last saw him—just a short six months ago—at the wedding. His usual bright pecan brown eyes were drawn. He had bags under his eyes. They looked distant and tired. Joey had always prided himself on his appearance.

His words rang in Miracle's head. "Chile, no, you always have to be dressed, never know who you may see. Can't let them see you slipping. Honey, they will be around town saying you're dipping."

"You are so crazy," I would always laugh.

"Child, boo… this is Atlanta, honey all about fake appearances here. You better ask somebody."

21

Mark walked over to the cabinet and retrieved a mug for Joseph, breaking Miracle's thoughts.

"You want your usual tea?"

"Yeah that's fine," Joseph responded.

"Miracle, you want a refill?"

"No, I'm good. I'll get some water in a minute."

It looked like Joseph had lost about 10 pounds. Joey was already slim, so he could not afford to lose an ounce. She felt it when she hugged him, but didn't say anything. He still had his muscle tone, but that would be gone soon, if he didn't put some weight back on quick.

"Sit tight. I'll get it. You two talk."

"Thanks, Mark."

Chapter Five

Joseph

"So, talk, that's why I'm here," Miracle said, as she smiled. "Okay, Joey. What happened to Tracey? I was just at your wedding six months ago."

Joseph looked away for a moment, and then turned his attention back to Miracle. He took a deep breath.

"Pneumonia," he moaned.

"Pneumonia," Miracle echoed. "I just talked to you last week and you never said Tracey was sick." She looked confused.

Mark cleared his throat. Joseph shot him a look.

"It's Miracle, Joseph, so stop playing games and tell her." Joey looked away again.

"She has a right to know the whole story. She's your sister—the only family who ever supports you. Don't do that."

Joseph started speaking in a low voice. He was barely audible.

"AIDS," Joey whispered.

"What!" Miracle exclaimed.

"AIDS," Joey repeated. "Goddamn AIDS!" he shouted this time.

Miracle gasped. She put her hand over her mouth. She was

speechless. She didn't know what to say. It was like the flood gates of heaven opened. The sobs and tears that emitted from Joseph's body broke Miracle's heart. The tears flowed like the Nile River. His ducts had finally been released. It was the first time he had said the word, since Tracey died. It hit him like a ton of bricks.

"How could a four letter word be so damn deadly? It has killed and shattered millions of lives. It's an awful disease. Why am I being punished?"

He knew why. *That happened so many years ago. I asked for forgiveness, so why am I paying for it now? It just doesn't seem fair. This was some bullshit.* Joseph was thinking to himself.

"Joey, how? When? And, why didn't you tell me?" Miracle's questions bought him back.

She had finally pulled herself together. She realized that now wasn't the time to fall apart. She was shocked, but she would have to deal with that later. Joey started speaking slowly again.

"We found out when we did the blood test for the marriage license. We knew before we got married, but we were optimistic that we could beat it. The meds were working and all was going well. However, about three months ago something changed, and things started going south. Tracey began getting sick and nothing helped. The doctors tried several different treatments, but to no avail—nothing. All they could do was make things comfortable from that point.

"We started doing hospice at home with an in-home nurse daily and I spent every possible waking moment with Tracey until the end."

Joey closed his eyes, as if remembering the moment. He took a few minutes before opening his eyes and speaking again.

"It's not right, Miracle. It just ain't right. Tracey was the most loving person in the world. Always happy, never complained, and he always saw the best in the worst people. Why did God take HIM? Can one person just answer that question for me? One damn person!"

Joseph was getting angry. He went from crying to being angry. He was all over the grief spectrum.

"Tracey! Tracey! Why! Why!" Joseph jumped up.

Miracle was rising to her feet to get him, but Mark waved her off. He mouthed to her to give him a minute. Joseph was now whimpering and rocking back and forth crying Tracey's name in a low voice. He was shaken to the core.

Joseph began remembering their first meeting. It seemed like only yesterday when he saw that fine specimen of a man, who walked into the meeting room. Joseph was meeting with a client, who was looking for an events coordinator to host the company's 10th Anniversary Celebration. It was a tech company that had come along at the right time. It was two geeky guys, who were roommates in college. They had invented this new coding program that would help companies solve some problem with something. Joey couldn't remember. He was never a computer guy. What he does remember was when the other partner walked in the room and was introduced, he had to contain himself.

"Joseph Jones, this is Tracey Thompson. He's my business partner. We were roommates in college."

Tracey extended his hand to Joseph and when their hands touched, electricity shot through Joseph's body.

"Nice to meet you, Joseph," Tracey smiled.

He had never experienced anything like that in his life. He was speechless for a second. And Joseph was never speechless.

"Are you ok?" Tracey asked.

Joseph swallowed, "Yes, I'm okay. I think, I just swallowed incorrectly," he coughed.

He was thinking. I'd like to swallow you.

"Nice to meet you Tracey," he finally managed to blurt out.

Joseph had sized up Tracey from head to toe. He was 6'3," 185-190 pounds and muscular. He had dirty blonde hair that hung over his black framed Ray Ban glasses. Those glasses were hiding the most crystal clear blue eyes he had ever seen. It was like looking into the ocean.

The Hugo Boss custom suit molded Tracey's body in all the right spots. The crisp white shirt with the red Ferragamo neck tie, sterling silver initial cuff links, manicured nails and a hint of Dolce and Gabbana Velvet Wood with Gucci shoes, almost took Joseph over the edge. Not only did the man look good, but he also smelled delicious. His teeth were those of a teenage braces candidate. There was nothing geeky about this guy at all. He was just Joseph's type. Well put together and fine.

Joseph, of course, later found out that Tracey didn't dress like this on a daily basis. The partners had a really important meeting later in the afternoon, after their meeting with him; and Tracey was forced to dress up. Tracey owned the attire, but rarely wore it—unless forced to. He preferred his Levi jeans, Polo shirts, loafers and maybe, an occasional khaki blazer. He wasn't a fancy dresser by any stretch of the means. However, he could pull it off, don't get it wrong. He was more comfortable in his jeans. Joseph grew to love it.

First impressions are everything; but sometimes they are not always what they appear. That was more than five years ago, but it seemed just like yesterday. It wasn't fair. It just wasn't fair that his sweet Tracey was gone.

They had been exclusive for four years, but because of the stupid laws; they weren't able to get married until six months ago and then he dies.

This is a living hell. Pure Hell! He breathed in fresh air to clear his mind.

I have so much to do Joseph was thinking. *Phone calls, funeral arrangements, obituary, clothes, etc.—too damn much. I still haven't even called Tracey's parents. I've tried.*

Joey's mind was full of thoughts that he couldn't utter out loud. *I've picked up the phone several times to dial their number, but I had to hang up each time. God knows I've tried. This is going to kill them. Tracey was their only child. He had a sister, but she died when they were kids. They had put everything into Tracey. They didn't care that he was gay. It didn't matter. He was their son. That's it, that's all!*

"Joey, earth to Joey," Miracle called out to get his attention.

She used to do that when they were kids, especially, when he would start daydreaming on her.

"Joey, where did you go? We lost you for a minute. Come sit back down, baby."

"I'm just thinking of all I have before me. I don't know

where to begin. I'm absolutely dreading contacting Tracey's parents. I still haven't told them. I tried, Mir. I picked up the phone a couple of times to call them, but I couldn't do it. It's going to kill them."

"Joey, it will hurt them more, if they hear it from a stranger. You have to tell them."

"I know, Mir, but I don't even know where to begin."

"You have to pull it together and call them."

Miracle got up and retrieved the cordless phone and handed it to Joseph.

"I'm right here. I got your back. Always have and always will."

"I know." Joey tried to smile.

"I love you, Mir. You are my Rock!"

Chapter Six

Karma

Karma refused to feel sorry for herself. Her heart felt a tinge of loneliness, but she refused to feel sorry for herself. There were people that she could call, like her brother, Mychal, to fill the void, but she just wasn't ready to deal with him, right now. Karma was learning to cope with her issues on her own. It was difficult, but she knows with God all things are possible. He was the only reason she could handle all of this. The nurse walked in and Karma plastered a smile on her face.

"How are you feeling, today, Mrs. Wright? I'm going to take your vitals," the nurse greeted her and smiled.

"The doctor put in an order for some tests. One of the techs should be around soon to take you down to have the test done. I'm going to go ahead and take your vitals and check your IV before you go down."

After the nurse finished checking her vitals, she observed, "You're continually smiling, so I guess that's good. I don't know how you do it. I have an attitude some days and don't want to be at work. You're the one lying in the hospital bed and you're smiling."

"One word," Karma responded. "JESUS!"

"If you don't know Him, you better get to know Him." Karma chuckled and added, "Honey, if I didn't know Him, I would be crazy after all the crap I just been through. He is the only reason I'm not in a mental hospital," Karma joked. "Jesus is my rock and my salvation. He gives me new faith and strength each day. I don't take any day for granted, any more. This illness has taught me to be forever grateful. We go through life unaffected by so much that surrounds us. It's terrible. It takes illness or death for us to stop and realize all that God has blessed us with throughout the years. Please don't get me on my soapbox, this morning," she beamed.

Karma continued, "People don't really want to hear it. If they did, the world would be a different place. Girl, finish taking these vital signs and get on out of here."

The nurse applied the blood pressure cuff to Karma's arm and placed the thermometer under her tongue. She noted Karma's vitals and checked the drip of the IV.

She was quiet while the nurse took her blood pressure and then responded, "You need to be thankful that God woke you up this morning to come to this job. Some people don't have a job and someone didn't wake up this morning."

"Dang, Mrs. Wright, you sure know how to make someone feel bad," she joked.

"I don't want you to feel bad. I want you to feel good and seek Him. That's my job as a Christian—to tell others about Him. As they say, 'I can lead you to the word, but I can't make you study it.'"

"I hear ya!" The nurse laughed. "Your vitals are good right now."

"That's because I'm talking about my God."

"The tech should be in soon. I'll check on you a little bit later. Thanks for the encouraging words!" She smiled as she went to visit her next patient.

Karma was still smiling, as she thought about the nurse. She pulled out her bible and started her bible study. She started with a prayer and asked God to lead her to a scripture today. She let the bible fall open on her lap and wherever it landed, she would study that for the day. It landed on Psalms 37… the Psalm of David.

The Bible verse read, *"Do not fret because of those who are evil or be envious of those who do wrong; for like the grass they will soon wither, like the green plants they soon die away. Trust in the Lord and do good; dwell in the land and enjoy safe pastures. Take delight in the Lord, and he will give you the desires of your heart…"* (Psalm 37: 1-4)

Karma laughed. This was one of her favorite scriptures.

How appropriate, you would land on that scripture today, she thought.

I don't need to go any further right now. I can move forward later. Those first four scriptures have enough meat in them by themselves. You already know all the evil that I've been faced with. It has turned my world upside down. The devil is busy. Every time I turn around it's something new— one thing after the other. But what does verse three say… Trust in the Lord.

"Thank you, Jesus!" she uttered out loud.

Tears started flowing down her cheeks. The average person would have gone crazy, if faced with what Karma was facing. She was so deeply rooted in her faith that she had no choice, but to move forward. Thanks to her praying grandmother all of those years ago, who made sure she knew the word. She strayed, but she always came back.

Do you know how hard it is to always smile, when you want to cry? She thought.

To laugh, when you want to fight.

Over the last year, Karma wanted to kill someone and had considered it a couple of times, but knew she could not handle prison. She always joked that she wasn't built to be Big Bertha's women in prison, so thank goodness Jesus had her back.

Lord, just have your way.

"Fix it Jesus and I will accept it, Father. Lord, I am leaning and depending on you. I'm ready, Lord. I'm ready."

The tears begin to come more frequent now, because Karma was at peace. Through the tears, she prayed, "Lord, please, protect my children, Father, guide them as they go through this life. Continue to keep them safe. Show them the way. Provide someone to help, lead and guide them along the way. Send my daughter a man who will protect and respect her, Lord. Let my sons become honorable men of society with decency, honesty and character. In Jesus' name, Amen."

Her children were the only area that Karma struggled with during this journey. The doctors had told her the only outcome was death. Karma knew she was going to die.

It was just a matter of when. Only God knew the date. She was ready though if that was His will. Her only regret would be not seeing her children become adults. That killed her more, day-by-day. She had two sons and a daughter. They were 19, 15 and 17, respectively. Seth, Brandon and Jessica were the only people that kept Karma fighting daily. She knew if it wasn't for them, she would have given up the fight by now. It was hard and the pain was unbearable, but when she saw their faces, she knew she would have to fight, if just for one more day. That is how she has made it for the past eight months. It has been a long road. The doctors keep telling her that she is a miracle. She typically responds by laughing and saying, "That's funny because my sister-in-law's name is Miracle. God sent her to me, so I guess that's my miracle."

Karma glanced back down at the bible. She reread verse four, "Take delight in the Lord, and he will give you the desires of your heart."

She wiped away her tears and smiled. Then, whispered, "Thank you, Father." Here is where my solace comes. I take delight in you and the desires of my heart will be given unto me. You already know what I desire before I even speak it. That's why I love you. I can lean and depend on you and you won't fail me. You're not like man. If I depended on man, then I surely would fail and so would my children, because my no good husband is a failure. He is so ugly and hateful. He must be from the pits of hell. Who does what he did? Only a snake would do that. I pray he rots in the fiery pits of hell.

Karma, stop it!

She had to catch herself. She was about to slip out of bible study and praising God that fast. The devil is busy and will creep in quick, if you let him. He doesn't have to use a lie. He can use the truth to knock you right off track. When you're praising the Lord and you surrender all, the devil doesn't like it at all.

"Forgive me, Father. That's another bible study."

Lord knows that craziness will make the hair on your neck stand straight up. I know I need to deal with it, but not today. I'm in a good place, right now. Not today. Lord, thank you for this time, this hour, and this study for what you will do for me wh…

The door opened and interrupted her.

"Mrs. Wright," a tech said sticking his head in the door.

"Yes," Karma replied.

"I'm here to take you down for the test the doctor ordered. Are you ready to go?"

"Ready as I'm going to get," she smiled and continued. "It's not like I'm going any place."

"Well, let's hit the road," he chuckled trying to keep the mood light. "This will be the best ride of your life," he joked.

"Really," Karma responded.

"Yes, Ma'am. They say I'm one of the best wheelchair drivers in this hospital. Ask anyone, they will tell you. I promise. From my mouth to God's ears," he grinned.

"You believe in God, young man?" Karma asked.

"Oh, yes, Ma'am. He's my rock. Don't do anything without him."

Karma knew she was in good hands and concluded, "Well, son, I know that this will be the best ride of my life. You're absolutely right. God is leading the way."

Karma smiled as the tech rolled her down the hall and she knew she would live to see at least one more day.

Chapter Seven

Mychal

Mychal hated when Miracle went away. He tried to act tough, like it didn't bother him, but it did. He was truly lost when she left the house. He was clueless. He didn't realize how much Miracle did until she was gone. He tried to pretend that he could handle it, but he couldn't even come close to doing what she did. He had no clue. He tried to protest when she said she would call Rosita to come while she was gone.

But inside, he was thinking, *please, let this woman call Rosita over here to help me.*

He would never part those juicy lips to say it, because he was a man and it would show weakness. Mychal would rather drown in failure, than ask for assistance.

Crazy, but true.

He was a big testosterone idiot. He was glad that Rosita was picking up the kids, taking them to their practices and bringing them home. He had left work early, so he could get home to be with Miracle's dad, but that was no biggie. He loved Patrick and they got along great. Miracle was worried about him, but Mychal didn't see anything wrong with him.

She was crazy at times worrying. She thought it was something wrong with him. If anything, she was the one with issues, Mychal grinned.

His cell phone rang. It was Miracle. Damn, that woman even knew when he was thinking bad about her. He shook his head and answered the phone through his car's Bluetooth.

"Hey, baby. I was just thinking about you," Mychal chuckled.

"Yeah, I bet," Miracle retorted.

"Naw, really, babe, I was."

"Whatever! Have you left work, yet?" she asked.

"Yes. I'm almost home."

"Did you stop and pick up dinner? Remember, I told you that Rosita wouldn't be able to cook tonight, because the kid's practices will be running late. I wanted dinner to be there when they got home.

"Uhm, uhm… yeah, baby I got…"

"Mychal, you're lying," Miracle said. She knew her husband like the back of her hand. When he started stuttering, she knew he was lying. Mychal was turning the car around, as she spoke.

"You're turning the car around, aren't you?"

"Nope," he lied.

"Uh huh…" she laughed.

He hated and loved that she knew him, so well. At times it was good, but at other times, it could be annoying. It did come in handy in some cases, when they were trying to get deals on stuff and they could bargain the heck out of sales people, because they knew what each other was thinking. But he hated it, because she knew when he was lying and could pull his card—immediately.

"Well, I placed the food order and it will be ready when you arrive. Don't flirt with your girlfriend behind the counter either," she teased.

"Really, Miracle," he shot back.

He hated when she teased him about this particular woman. She was butt ugly. The women always flirted with him and he tried to be nice, but he hated it. Her flirting made him feel really uncomfortable.

"Anyway," Miracle said with a chuckle, "Call me later,

when you get home. I have to go."

"Yeah, later," he sarcastically added, and then ended the call.

Damn that woman can get under my skin at times. Mychal turned up Kem on the radio, and hoped home girl wasn't working today, when he reached the restaurant.

Of course, his prayers weren't answered. Butt ugly was the first thing he saw when he walked in the door. She was smiling from ear-to-ear revealing her two front gold teeth. Her hair was pulled up so high in a hard crisp Mohawk. It looked like they used the whole can of hair spray or whatever women use to keep their hair together. She waved at Mychal as he walked in. At least she wasn't behind the 'To Go' counter. She was waiting on a table. Mychal did a quick wave and walked briskly to the 'To Go' counter. He wanted to get the hell out of there fast, before she made her way over there. Mychal passed by a couple of tables and a beautiful woman laughing at a table over in the corner caught his eye. Her angelic laugh stopped him briefly for a moment. She was breathtaking. Her skin was the color of a caramel apple with the same smoothness. Her skin was flawless and her makeup was perfectly placed. Mychal smiled and his mind almost started wandering, but he pulled it back. He had never cheated on Miracle and wasn't the type of husband who would; however, he was still a man. When he saw a nice looking woman, his mind wandered to those videos that he secretly watched in the middle of the night, while his family was sleep. He liked fantasizing about doing some of those moves with different women. He would never act on it, but he had a great imagination.

What man didn't, right?

What he saw next stopped his fantasy dead in the tracks! His eyes were following the woman's slim hands and they were connected to some big dark working hands that belonged to a familiar face—Walter, his brother-in-law.

What the fuck?

Mychal fumed to himself. He rubbed his eyes to make sure he was seeing correctly. Yeah, it was that bama. He was sitting there, engulfed in some story and now, the young lady was not nearly as beautiful. Yes, she was still fine, but some of her beauty had waned.

Anyway, what the hell was he doing in a restaurant, tucked away in the corner with some woman, other than my sister, and holding her hand?

It took everything in his power to stop himself from charging right over to the table and asking that very question—but he contained himself. He pulled his cell phone out and started snapping pictures. He pretended to be fiddling with his phone. However, he had to do some more investigating, before opening up 'a can of whip ass' on good ole' Walter. Don't get it twisted, he could definitely whip that ass, but he didn't want to do anything—prematurely.

Maybe it wasn't what it appeared to be.

Mychal was a civil man—he tried to give people the benefit of the doubt, most of time. He had come a long way. He had worked hard at leaving his past behind. He didn't want to wake up the lion. Yes, let the sleeping lion lie, because once it roars, it isn't pretty.

"I got my eye on you, Walter. Bet your ass, I do," he mumbled.

This is some crazy shit. I come to pick up some damn food and I see this. I tell you everything is for a reason. See that's why as much as you may think about it, fellows, it's not worth it. I'm sure, he figured he would get away with it, since he's an hour away from his home. But Big Brother is always watching and just when you think no one sees, someone does. This bama, right here, got some nerve.

Pull it together Mychal, he told himself.

He could start to feel his collar getting hot. The couple at the table that Mychal stopped next to started staring at him. He didn't want to cause a disruption in the restaurant, nor risk the chance of Walter seeing him; so, he quickly walked to the 'To Go' counter, paid for the food and left the restaurant.

He wanted to call Miracle back so bad and tell her what he saw, but he decided against it. He would wait until she got back. He wasn't sure what she was dealing with in Atlanta with Joey. Besides, he wanted to see the reaction on her face, when he showed her the pics. Miracle made the best facial expressions. He had told her on several occasions that she could never be a professional poker player. Her bluff would get called all the time. Walter, better be glad that his bluff didn't get called in this damn restaurant.

I would have tossed his ass around like this salad in this bag.

Mychal started his car and headed home.

Patrick was watching CNN.

"Dad," Mychal called out.

"In here, son," Patrick called. "I'm in the media room."

"How's it going, Dad? How was your day?"

"Good, son. Real good. How about yours?" Patrick asked. "You look like you got something on your mind."

Mychal sat down in one of the leather recliner chairs next to his father-in-law.

"Naw, I'm good," Mychal lied. He was still replaying that scene from the restaurant in his head. It played over and over again on the ride home. He saw the women laughing, then Walter.

"You sure, son? You know you can talk to me. Trust me, I know my daughter is a hand full to deal with at times. Remember, I was married to her mother. The apple doesn't fall far from the tree," Patrick laughed.

Mychal smiled. "No, that's not it, Dad. Not this time, at least. It was a long day at work. We're working on these new proposals trying to land a new big project across town and it's a little stressful. Nothing I can't handle, but still stress, no less."

"If you say so, son," Patrick responded.

"You want a beer, Dad?"

"Naw, son. I'm trying to catch up on this news. I need a clear head to listen to this bull crap. They always trying to blame President Obama for everything that goes wrong in America, nowadays. It's crazy! Maybe, later."

"Yeah, you're right. I should go workout, anyway. It helps to relieve stress."

"Talking does, too," Patrick smirked and turned his attention back to the news. Mychal wondered why Miracle thought this man was losing his mind. He seemed fine; he still had his wit and intuition. He was just getting old. Miracle was paranoid.

"Your absolutely right, dad, talking does help, but for me sweating helps even more." Mychal laughed and walked out of the media room.

He should be able to get a quick couple of miles in before Rosita got home with the kids.

Mychal loved running. It cleared his head. It let him be mindless. He was tired of thinking. It was nice to have a time, when he could just relax, run and not think.

Mychal had always been an athlete. He was a natural at any sport he tried, but he gravitated towards basketball and baseball. Basketball won his heart and paid for his college education. Mychal got a full-ride to college from his basketball ability.

Thanks to a neighborhood coach and his keen eye to notice how Mychal was a natural. He mentored Mychal and never asked for anything in return, other than Mychal return the same for another young man, after he made it. Mychal broke so many records and had colleges scouting him in middle school. By the time he made it to high school, they were on him like white on rice. Colleges wanted him to leave school in the 10th grade, but his parents would not hear of it.

He remembered his father saying, "No, indeed. If they want you that bad now, just think how much more they will really want you in two years. Education is first in this house—always has been and always will be. There is no way in hell that Mychal Alexander will not finish high school, while living in the Alexander household. I don't give a damn, how good you are!"

Then, his dad would add, "Unless Jesus, himself, tells me to let you go to the NBA, then you will be right there at Central High School, until you walk across that stage. Dad knows best."

Mychal later realized how much his dad was right. He did make it to college, the NBA and played for about five seasons, but he got hurt and never fully recovered from his injury. He was medically retired from the NBA and just like his dad had told him—he had to fall back on the education that his father made him obtain.

"Nothing in life is a guarantee, son. Trust me, that is one thing, you can take to the bank." Mr. Alexander would always tell him.

His dad would continue to keep Mychal grounded, while rising to stardom. He was his good angel on the right shoulder. He was sure his son had the devil angel on the left; however, he spoke loud enough to drown the devil out. Mychal slipped at times, but for the most part he did listen and of course, the reason he is successful to this day. If it wasn't for his dad, he knows that he could have ended up like a lot of those cats out there who had it all—and lost it all— because they didn't have anyone in their corner mentoring them through the process. There are a lot of snakes in the business, and if you're not careful you will get bit; and sometimes the venom kills. Mychal appreciated his dad's concern. He may not have understood it then, but he understands now and he thanks his dad, quite often. He takes care of his parents, well. They want for nothing.

Mychal threw on his running gear; synchronized his Apple watch; slid on his Beats headphones; and headed out the door. He would just do a quick run, since the kids would be home soon and he wanted to be back, so they could have dinner together, since Miracle wasn't at home. It was rare that the kids ate without one of them present. They agreed at least one parent would be present for dinner time. They preferred both, but at least one must be there unless, they were out of town together. It gave them time to find out what was going on with the kids and have a little family time over dinner. Of course, more times than not, it was Miracle, because her job was more flexible and she often worked from home. Mychal made every effort to be there, as well. He enjoyed having dinner with his family. It usually turned into something funny or off the wall, especially, since Patrick joined the family dynamics. His father-in-law was hilarious.

The nice breeze climbed across Mychal's face as he headed down the street. The air bought a smile to his face, then, he thought about the scene from the restaurant.

He saw the women's face and her hand in Walter's hand.

What was the deal?

First of all, she was way too beautiful to be with Walter, so there's no way he's intimate with her. I can't believe that for a second.

Now, if it was me, then yes.

Mychal smiled to himself. Mychal had a touch of arrogance about himself, but he wasn't an ass about it. He was an attractive man and he knew it. Others knew it, too. He didn't thrive on the fact, but still he was confident and a little cocky at times.

Mychal would have to call his sister; better yet, he would go see her. He suddenly realized it had been months, since they had seen each other. He was so busy with work and life. It was no excuse though. She only lived about an hour away. They used to spend a lot of time together, but lately he just let life get in the way. He knew that Miracle and Karma spoke more frequently and had been shopping a few times. He was going to make it a point to see her. Seeing Walter with that woman triggered something, and he knew something wasn't quite right.

He had always been her big brother. Her protection when she was out of the presence of their dad. Between him and his dad, they didn't let anything happen to her. They would kill someone dead, if they messed with that girl. People knew it, too.

People used to say, "That's the Alexander girl. You'd better not mess with her. Her dad and brother will kill you. They are crazy when it comes to that girl."

He remembers once, some new boy moved into the neighborhood and he pushed his sister down and took her bike. She came home crying and her knees were bloody. Mychal was in the yard playing basketball, of course.

"What happened?"

"The new boy pushed me down and took my bike."

"What?" Mychal yelled.

"He took my new bike."

"Where's he at?"

"I don't know," she said. "He rode off with it."

"Okay. Let's go," he said.

They walked out the yard and low and behold, guess who was riding down the street on her bike… the new boy. Mychal ran behind him and caught up to him. By this time all of the neighborhood kids started crowding around, because they knew what was about to happen.

Some were yelling, "I told you not to take her bike. You messed up, now."

"You about to get your butt kicked," someone else yelled.

Mychal kicked the boy straight off the bike. He went flying across the street and the bike hit the ground. The mirror and one of the reflector lights shattered on the ground. His sister was standing there still with tears in her eyes. The boy groaned as he hit the ground.

The crowd roared, "Get him, Mychal! Get him." They were screaming.

Mychal took one look at the boy and saw he was scared to death. He walked over and helped him up off the ground.

"Look, man, this is my sister and I know you just moved here, but don't nobody mess with my sister. Got it?"

"Yeah, I got it," the new boy murmured in pain.

Mychal grinned as he took his next stride remembering the story, because the boy became his best friend; and actually, dated his sister. He thought they were going to get married, but she ended up with that damn Walter—a whole other story.

I wonder why Karma didn't call me. He thought. He knew why, laughing. He would have went ape shit on Walter. But I will get to the bottom of this.

You bet your ass, I will. He said to himself.

Mychal turned up his music and let his mind flow free of Walter, whatever Miracle was dealing with Joseph and anything else that may be brewing. He just wanted to hear the music and feel the tension of his muscles, as they contracted and relaxed with each beat of the concrete. He was headed back home to shower, and then have dinner with his family. He would focus on everything else another day.

Chapter Eight

Mychal

Mychal was walking down the steps and headed to the kitchen, just as the kids and Rosita were walking in the door.

"Hey, Dad," Mason and McKenzie said at the same time and they ran past him up the steps.

"Hey, where y'all going?" Mychal responded.

"I have homework," McKenzie said.

"I need to get on the computer," Mason replied.

"Dinner is in ten minutes; it just needs to be warmed up. Please, don't make me call you again."

"Okay," they both responded.

Mychal already knew it wasn't going to happen. Rosita or he would be screaming back up the steps again, in ten minutes. Mychal continued down the stairs.

"Hola, Mr. Alexander," Rosita chimed.

"Hola, Rosita."

"Como estas?" Rosita asked.

"Muy bien. Y tú?" Mychal responded.

"Muy bien," Rosita replied. "You're getting good," Rosita laughed.

"I'm trying," he laughed back.

"Just keep practicing and you'll get it."

"I don't know about that Rosita."

"You will. Mrs. Alexander said that you were picking up dinner."

"Yes, I was on my way to the kitchen. It's on the counter. I decided to go for a quick run, when I got home from work."

"No worries, Mr. Alexander, go relax. I will take care of it. Just give me a few minutes. I will get everything warmed up and put it out on the table. Will your father be joining you?" Rosita asked with a slight smirk.

He smiled, "Yes, Rosita."

"Okay, señor."

Rosita wanted to hurry up and get out of there, before she saw Patrick. He always gave her a hard time. She didn't know why, but he did. He liked making fun of her accent and always had something to say about Spanish people. Of course, Rosita never said anything, because she didn't want to risk losing her job, but she feared one day that Mr. Patrick would catch her on the wrong day and her Spanish heritage would come out and she would go off on him. For now, she just bit her tongue and dealt with it. Mrs. Alexander always said something to her father, but it still didn't stop him from making comments, every so often. Rosita knew he would try to make some smart remarks. She decided to just ignore him, if he did. Hopefully, she could get the food ready and get out the door before she saw him.

Rosita was almost to the kitchen.

"Buenos Dias, Rosita."

She heard Patrick's voice and froze for a moment. Even the sound of that man's voice made her cringe.

"It's Buenos Noches," she responded. "Dias is day. Noches is night," she explained.

"Whatever!" Patrick said. "It's all the same," he laughed. She shook her head and kept walking into the kitchen.

"Dad!" Mychal exclaimed. "Don't start. I'm going to tell Miracle. Please, don't make me call her, right now and tell her that you are giving Rosita a hard time, already. Damn."

"I was just trying to speak," Patrick responded. "She's so damn sensitive and you sound like a chump talking about you going to call my daughter to tell on me. You new-age husbands," Patrick laughed. "I'm going to tell Miracle," Patrick mocked.

Mychal shot him a look. "Dad, please! You know better. Miracle just told me to call her if you start giving Rosita a hard time. But trust me, I can handle you. I know, you know, I can."

They did a stare down and then both laughed.

"You right, son. No point in calling Miracle."

Patrick talked a good game, but he didn't want Mychal to pick up the phone. He knew Miracle would dig into his tail for messing with Rosita, because she specifically told him, before she left, not to do it.

These two always played tough, but they knew who was the glue holding this family together—Miracle. Hands down! No ifs, ands, or buts about it.

"Go get ready for dinner," Mychal told him. "It should be ready in a few minutes. Rosita is getting it together now. Miracle called in an order from our favorite place and I picked it up on the way home."

Really! Mychal said to himself when Patrick walked into the powder room.

That old man is funny. Maybe he is losing his mind. Going to try to punk me in my own house; he better be glad I love him and he's Miracle's dad. I would have lit that old ass up in here. Mychal chuckled.

Calling me a chump, no, sir. Whew, I know I've changed.

Thank you, Lord. Only you kept me from opening that can of whip ass and being able to laugh about it. Only You! He smiled.

Mychal called up to Mason and McKenzie, "Let's go, time to eat," just as they were coming down the steps.

Rosita came out of the kitchen and said, "Okay, Mr. Alexander, I set everything up. I'll be in the kitchen getting ready for tomorrow. Let me know, if you need anything. When you guys are done, I'll put the dishes in the dishwasher, and then I'm going to head home. I'll see you all in the morning, unless you need me to stay?"

"No, Rosita, we should be okay. That will be fine. We'll see you in the morning."

"Bueno…" Patrick started to say something.

Mychal shot him a look and he stuffed his fork in his mouth.

"Dios Mio!" Rosita rolled her eyes and walked away.

"How was practice, Mason?" Mychal interjected trying to change the subject.

"It was cool, dad. We did a couple of new plays to get ready for the game this weekend, but for the most part, things pretty much were the same. You know they need me." He laughed and patted his chest.

"They do? Huh! Mighty funny the coach sat your butt down almost a whole quarter, when you screwed up at the last game."

"Naw, dad, it was whack, because it wasn't my fault. Coach be geeking."

"First of all, speak English when you're speaking to me, because I don't know what half of the stuff means that you just said."

McKenzie snickered. "Dad, you need to get with the new lingo," she giggled.

"No, you all need to learn to speak proper English. Now, let's try that again."

"Dad, I'm just saying, it wasn't right. I didn't mess up that time; it was Jason. He screwed up the assist and coach thought it was me. I paid for someone else, who messed up."

"Okay, you may be right, but it was your mouth that got you in trouble. I tell you all the time, 'loose lips, sink ships,' but you don't believe me. You will learn one day. You'll learn."

Mychal saw so much of himself in his son—it was scary. The boy was good. Not as good as he was, but he was good. He needed to work on his mouth and temper. If he could line those two up with his talent, he would be unstoppable. Hopefully, he could stay healthy and go further than he did. It was a hurtful thing, when he couldn't play in the NBA any more, but oh, well, there is life after the NBA.

"Dad," McKenzie snapped him back.

"Yes, baby, what's up?"

"You didn't ask me about dance class."

"You didn't give me a chance. I was talking to your brother. I was going to ask you next. How was class?" He smiled broadly.

His eyes lit up when he talked to his baby girl. He couldn't believe she was already fifteen. It seemed like yesterday when she was born. She was the other leading lady in his life, behind his wife. She was his precious baby girl. He felt sorry for the man coming to ask for her hand in marriage. The brother better be on point. Mychal didn't play when it came to the women in his life. He would protect them to the end. He may lack in other areas, but protection and safety was not one of them.

"Taylor was doing the routine all wrong," McKenzie stated. "She's so uncoordinated. She goes the wrong way all the time. Our instructor gets so frustrated. She keeps telling her to practice, but I don't think she does."

"Well, maybe you should ask her if she needs help, Kenzie."

"What? I'm not helping her, dad. I don't even like her," McKenzie retorted.

"Kenzie, that's not nice. We didn't raise you like that. You're supposed to help others in need," Mychal responded.

McKenzie scrunched up her face.

"What's that for?"

"Dad, when did you become so righteous? I remember you telling mommy you couldn't stand Mr. Greene down the street."

"That's something different, Kenzie," he replied.

"Uh huh, adults kill me saying stuff is different for them."

"Sounds the same to me," Patrick chimed in.

Mychal shot him a look again. He stuck the fork in his mouth, again.

Mason cracked up laughing. He added, "I think, they got you on this one, dad," Mason choked through his laughs.

Mychal tried to think of a comeback, but was stuck. "Hurry up and finish eating, so you can get done with your homework and get ready for bed."

He needed Miracle; she would've known how to respond. *Damn, she got me,* he thought.

McKenzie and Mason looked at each other and grinned. They loved to see their dad squirm.

"How was your day, grandpa?" McKenzie turned her attention to her grandpa. She knew how far to go with her dad. She had hit the nail, but she knew better than to hammer it in. It wouldn't end pretty. She figured she better move on to safer ground, which was grandpa.

"It was great, sweetie. Same old shit, just a different day."

McKenzie snickered. She loved her grandpa so much. He was just raw. He didn't care. He held his tongue for no one. He had no filter. Whatever came up, came out. She got a kick out of it, because it drove her mother crazy. Her mom was all prim and proper, so grandpa was a hoot and it was even better when mom was around.

"I just caught up on some world news and the crap of people blaming the president for all of the world's problems. Other than that, it was okay," Patrick affirmed.

"Glad you had a good day," McKenzie smiled.

"Me, too," he replied.

"You coming to my game this weekend, grandpa?" Mason asked.

"God willing," he responded. "Unless, He takes me home before then to meet Elizabeth, I'll be there." Patrick joked grabbing his chest.

"Who is Elizabeth, Grandpa?" McKenzie asked.

"She should have been your grandmother," he laughed.

"Huh?" McKenzie asked confused.

"Are you guys done?" Mychal interjected. "It's getting late. Go ahead and take your plates into the kitchen, so Rosita can get done and go home for the evening."

"But who is Elizabeth, Dad?" McKenzie asked still confused.

"Grandpa is just being silly, baby. Don't pay him any mind. You know how your grandpa is always joking." Mychal just shook his head.

This man was really pushing him to the limits, today. What was going on with him?

Mason and McKenzie got up and took their plates into the kitchen.

"I was just having some fun with my grandbabies," Patrick snorted.

"Okay, if you say so, dad," Mychal responded. "But I bet, Miriam wouldn't think it was funny, talking about Elizabeth should've been their grandmother. She should come in and haunt you tonight in your sleep for talking ill of the dead. Your wife loved you with all of her heart. You're a mess. I love you, but you're a mess. What are we going to do with you? I'm going to go find a comedy club to put you on stage, since you got so many jokes. Maybe you missed your calling. You know, it's never too late to start a new career."

"Jokes for seniors… real funny," Patrick pointed out.

Chapter Nine

Patrick

Patrick was sitting on his bed thinking, *Shoot maybe I should go tell some jokes.*

I'm funny. Hell, I'm not doing nothing else. Miracle won't let me do anything. I can sneak out at night and get on stage and make some folks laugh. I still got it. I know I'm funny. I keep people laughing anyway; I might as well do something with it. Yeah, why not? Mychal was trying to be funny, but tomorrow, I'm going to look up some clubs and see what an old man can do. They trying to count me out, just because I'm getting old. I ain't dead. I got plenty of life left in me.

Patrick looked over at the nightstand and picked up a picture of him and Miriam. He smiled at the memory of his wife. He missed her so much. He never imagined that she would die before him. She was a sweet woman.

Patrick reminisced about the old times… years ago. It was as plain in his mind, as if it happened yesterday… He loved her from the moment he saw her. He knew that she would be his wife. They got married and never looked back. It was different back then—that was the norm. What wasn't normal was that Miriam was engaged to someone else and was to be married to him in two months, but Patrick couldn't let that happen. She was the love of his life and he would go to any lengths to make sure he had Miriam and not anyone else. Patrick and Miriam had gone to the same elementary and middle school, but then her family moved away. They were like Frick and Frack the whole time they attended school together. Miriam didn't think of Patrick like that though. Her daddy was strict and she couldn't even think of boys. She was young any way. However, Patrick loved her from first sight.

When they moved away, he was heartbroken, but he vowed he would find her and marry her. Well, as the years passed after they moved away, he never could find her.

Finally, a woman from the neighborhood, who was still friends with Miriam's family, had received an invitation to the wedding. The women came into the general store where Patrick worked to find a gift. He overheard the woman saying she needed a gift for the Miriam girl that used to live in the neighborhood. She was getting married in Philadelphia and the woman was so excited about going, because she had never been there. Patrick stopped dead in his tracks and almost dropped the stock in his hands.

He thought, *It can't be. No way.*

Patrick scooted a little closer, so he could hear the lady a little better.

Was he hearing this right?

"I needs something real special. I've known that girl since she was a baby," the lady stated. "I'm's just so excited to be going to Philadelphia, I can't stand it. Thank the Lord, that my first cousin's sister lives there, so I have a place to stay," the lady added.

"Child, cuz if not, I wouldn't be able to go and that would just break my heart not to see her get married."

Patrick was thinking, You *still might not be seeing her get married.*

He knew that he had to get to Philadelphia quick to find out if this was his Miriam. He wondered when the wedding was.

"When is the wedding?" his co-worker asked.

Yes, he thought.

"It's in two months, but you knows I'm on a budget and I just so happened to get some extras money this month, so I figured I should come on in and find something now, so I wouldn't have to worry about it later. I'm just goin' keep it wrapped up 'til I's ready to go," she said.

Patrick had to figure out what he was going to do, but he knew it was no way that he was not going to Philadelphia to at least try to look for Miriam. He had lost her once, and he wasn't going to lose her, again. He didn't care who she was about to marry. He was about to quit his job anyway, because he had already gone down and signed up to join the Marines. They had given him a deployment date in two months. He had two months to convince Miriam that it was him she wanted to marry. He was crazy. She probably didn't even remember him. It had been years. Of course, she did. They were best friends since five.

She was going to be his wife. He decided that he was going to quit his job and just head to Philadelphia, until he had to report to Montford Point at Camp Lejeune in North Carolina. He had been saving his money, since he had been working at the general store, so the money was covered. He had family in Philadelphia, and he hoped he could stay with them, so he wasn't worried about it. He didn't care. He would sleep anywhere, as long as he found Miriam.

Patrick finished his work for the day and went to his boss.

"Can I talk to you, sir?" Patrick asked.

"What is it, Patrick?" Mr. Alston questioned.

Patrick hated doing this, but he had no choice. His boss had been the only person who would give him a job. He saw something in Patrick and decided to take a chance on him.

"Well, sir, Uhm, I…"

"What is it, Patrick? What's the matter? Did something happen? Did someone treat you bad or say something wrong to you?"

"No, sir, not at all."

Mr. Alston didn't accept improper behavior in his place of business. Everyone was treated fairly.

"Just say it."

"I really appreciate you giving me this job and all, Mr. Alston, you know I'm about to go into the Marines; but I just found out that a… well… a girl that I love… lost… many years ago, is living in Philadelphia. I know this sounds crazy, but I need to go find her."

Mr. Alston just starred at Patrick for a minute, and then he grinned. He understood. He was a hopeless romantic himself and had married his high school sweetheart after many protests from her parents, so he knew what it felt like.

He patted Patrick on his shoulder and said, "I understand. I will be sorry to lose you and I thought I would have two months to find someone to replace you, but trust me, I understand. I tell you what, I will pay for you to get to Philadelphia," Mr. Alston said.

"It's the least I can do for all the hard work you did around here. You always stayed when I asked you and went the extra mile. I truly appreciate it. Patrick, it will be hard to replace you. You will be a true asset to the Marines and I know they will turn you into a decent man."

"OO-RAH!" Patrick shouted. "Mr. Alston, you don't have to do that," Patrick said.

"I know I don't have to do it. I want to do it. Now, get on out of here and get your stuff together, so you can get to Philadelphia. Come by in the morning and I will have your bus ticket. Take care of yourself, Patrick, and make me and your country proud."

"Thank you, sir."

"Thank you."

Patrick couldn't believe it. Things went better than he thought. He was so nervous, but it worked out. Now, he had to convince his mother that he wasn't crazy. He was going, no matter what. Maybe he would just tell her that the Marines called him to North Carolina early. Yeah, he would do it. It was only a little white lie. He hated lying to his mother, but he had little time and no choice.

Patrick ran into the house and his mother was in the kitchen cooking. He was sweating. He had run all the way home, he was so excited.

"Hey, mama!"

"What's wrong with you?" she said. "Who you running from? What you dun, boy?"

"Nothing, mama."

"Den why you running? Black boys ain't running round here in lessin' they den dun something."

"Mama, please! Stop worrying. I haven't done anything. I'm just happy."

"What you so happy 'bout?" she asked.

"Well, uhm, remember, I told you I was going to the Marines. They told me I can start tomorrow. So, I'm going to Philadelphia tomorrow to start training."

"D'mrrow?" his mother said. "I thought you won't be leavin' for two months."

"I know mama, but they told me to come early."

He kept moving around. He couldn't look his mother straight in the eyes, because she knew when he was lying.

"I got to go pack my stuff, mama."

He walked off hastily to the room he shared with his two younger brothers. Patrick could hardly contain himself. He was giddy and scared at the same time.

He wanted to find Miriam more than anything in the world, but he was afraid of going to a new city and fearful he wouldn't find her. He had to believe it was his destiny.

Patrick got off the bus in Philadelphia and couldn't believe his eyes. It was totally different than his little hometown. His mother had given him his family's information, so he just had to figure out where the heck it was. He guessed he would have to take the local bus, but didn't want to pull out his money. It was tucked away in the hidden pocket his mom had sewn in his pants before he left.

Patrick shrugged his shoulders and began to walk. He wanted to see the sites anyway. It was exciting to him to be in a big city. Patrick saw some of the tallest buildings he had ever seen. He was amazed. He was so caught up in the sites that he didn't realize he had been walking for over an hour. Patrick was so thirsty.

He saw a store called F. W. Woolworth Company and went in to grab something to drink. Patrick walked in and his eyes widened. This looked nothing like the general store he was used to back home. This place was huge. It had everything. They even had a food/lunch counter. His stomach began to growl. He didn't even realize he was hungry. His mom had packed him some food for the bus trip, but he had eaten it all hours ago. Patrick walked closer to the counter and walked up and down, but wasn't sure if he could sit down. He didn't see the sign.

Just then he heard a voice, "You want to sit down and order something to eat?"

He looked up and couldn't believe it. It was Miriam.

"Uhm, Uhm," he almost whispered and he couldn't believe his eyes.

Was this really her right here before him?

"Miriam. Are you Miriam?" he asked.

"Yes, how did you know my name?" she said. "Oh, my uniform says it," she smiled.

She was still pretty as ever.

"I forgot it was on there. I just started working here," she confessed. "My parents didn't want me to take this job, but I did anyway. I want to make my own money and be independent," she whispered.

Patrick was frozen. He didn't know what to do or say.

"Are you ok?" she asked. "Can I get you something to drink?"

"Uhm, Uhm, water, please."

"Ok, coming up. We have a meatloaf special today, just to

let you know. Be right back with your water."

She walked away leaving Patrick sitting there looking like a lost puppy. He needed to snap out of it quick.

Get it together—Patrick. You have traveled all this way to find this girl and she is right here and now you are freezing up. Are you serious? You don't have time for this, man.

"Here's your water. Did you want to order something to eat?"

"Uhm, Uhm."

"Are you sure you okay?" Miriam asked.

Patrick finally got his words out. "Yeah, I'm okay. I'll take the meatloaf special, it sounds good. It's just been a long day," he declared.

"I guess," she smiled. "One meatloaf order coming up," Miriam said. Another person had walked up to the other end of the counter and sat down.

"I'm going to place your order and be back," Miriam informed him.

She walked down to the other customer. A few minutes later Miriam was coming back with Patrick's meatloaf plate.

It's now or never stop being scared, he told himself. Miriam sat the meatloaf plate down.

"Can I ask you a question?"

"Sure, shoot," Miriam sputtered and then looked at him strangely.

"Did you go to Dunbar Elementary and Carver Middle School?" Patrick asked.

Miriam's eyes widened. "Yes," Miriam replied hesitantly. "Why?"

"It's me, Patrick," he responded. "I can't believe you don't remember me. How could you forget me? We were best buds back then," he laughed.

She looked at him. "Oh, my goodness, Patrick. I would have never thought in a million years that I would see you here. What are you doing here? It's been so long. How did you even know it was me?" she asked curiously.

"I could never forget you, Miriam. You were my best friend for all those years and you haven't changed one bit," he grinned.

"Well, you sure have," Miriam said before she realized it. "I mean. You look different," she corrected. "You used to be a scrawny, little skinny kid," she chuckled.

"I'm not scrawny, anymore," Patrick shot back.

Miriam smiled and quickly turned away. Her face went a little red.

He sure wasn't, she thought.

She hadn't seen Patrick in years. She was so upset when her family moved all those years ago. She felt like her world had been turned upside down. She did think of him every day, when they first moved, but as time passed, so did her thoughts.

"So?" Miriam said. "Why are you here? I know you didn't come all the way to Philadelphia to sit in Woolworth's and order meatloaf," she joked.

Patrick laughed. "No, I didn't come to sit in Woolworth's and order meatloaf, but it's a good thing I did. I came here to find you."

"Me! What do you mean you came to find me? After all these years?" she looked puzzled. "How did you even know I would be here?" she asked.

"I didn't," Patrick smiled. "I got lucky. Call it what you want luck, destiny, meatloaf or whatever. I don't care. All I know is that I found you."

Miriam was confused. She had no idea what Patrick was talking about or why after all this time, he was here. It was good to see him, but she was totally lost.

Chapter Ten

Miracle

Miracle convinced Joey to lie down, again.

They reached out to Tracey's parents, which was very draining. It broke her heart to hear them on the line. Tracey's mom let out the loudest scream Miracle thought she had ever heard in her life. Tracey's father was silent. He probably was in shock. It took him several minutes to respond.

Finally, he spoke and said that they would be in Atlanta, as quickly as possible.

They lived in Seattle. Joseph told Miracle that they owed a beautiful home on the water there. Joseph loved going there to visit. He said that it transferred him from the hustle and bustle of Atlanta. It was a peaceful and serene getaway. Maybe Joey could visit for a while after everything was over to get some time away and help him begin to heal.

Miracle tried to get Joey to start talking about funeral arrangements after they spoke with Tracey's parents, but Joseph broke into tears and couldn't stop crying. He just sat, stared and cried. She decided it was best he rest for a while and they could try again tomorrow. It was getting late anyway and she wanted to check in on the home front.

Miracle was in the lavishly decorated guest room sitting in the cream colored high-backed wing chair. The room was burnt orange and eggplant with splashes of cream and black accented throughout. It made her think of royalty. She thought she had an eye for color, but man, Joey, had her beat. His esthetic was genius. She proudly smiled.

She dialed Mychal's cell number.

"Hello."

"Hey, babe," Miracle greeted.

"What's up, sweetie" Mychal hummed back. "How's it going? What is going on down there? I thought, I would have heard from you earlier. I was just about to call you."

"Mychal, I don't even know where to begin," she responded.

"You can begin by telling me why in the hell your brother called our house disturbing me in the middle of the damn night," he said.

"Mychal," she yelled into the phone. "Don't do that. That's not nice."

"Well, not nice, but true, so let's start there."

Miracle rolled her eyes. *This man,* she thought.

"It's Tracey. Tracey is dead."

"Dead?" Mychal stated sounding confused.

"Yes, dead," Miracle repeated.

"I thought they just got married six months ago. What happened? Was it an accident? Geez. I'm sorry, Miracle," he said softly. "I just assumed, it was another one of Joseph's crazy rants."

"You know, how he is."

"Well, of course, you do, he's your brother. How is he?"

"Not good," Miracle answered. "He's not taking this well, at all. He is trying to sleep right now. He just told Tracey's parents a bit ago. They are making arrangements to get here. It was one of the most difficult things to watch, since my mother's death. I feel so helpless to Joey. I don't know what to do."

"Just being there speaks volumes. I'm sure he appreciates you dropping everything and coming when he called, as you always do. Babe, you know what to do. It's in your blood. That's why everyone calls on you."

Miracle pulled the phone away from her ear and glanced at the screen to make sure she was still talking to Mychal.

Was this Mychal Alexander saying this?

"Have you been drinking, Mychal?" she asked.

He started laughing. "No, babe, I have not been drinking."

Miracle didn't know where this was coming from. Mychal usually got mushy and appreciative when he had a couple of drinks.

She hadn't been gone long enough for things to quite fall apart yet, so she was thinking, *Who was this guy? Wow, maybe she should start leaving home more often, if it was going to cause this reaction.*

"Hello!" Mychal called into the phone. "Miracle, are you still there?"

"Yeah, I'm here," Miracle said. "Just trying to figure out what happened to my husband!" She exclaimed. "It's obvious, he has been abducted and some other person is in my home right now, pretending to be him," she chuckled.

"Woman, please! I got your abduction," he joked. "Seriously, how is Joseph? I can't believe it. I remember it like it was yesterday, when you flew down there for the wedding and now you are there helping him plan a funeral. Shit!" Mychal proclaimed.

"Mychal," Miracle screamed. "You know, I don't like it when you use profanity."

"I'm a grown-ass man," Mychal piped.

"I know it, but I still don't like it."

"Sorry, babe… but damn this situation is enough to make you cuss and drink. How is he doing?"

"Not good at all. Mark had to call the doctor to give him something to calm down his nerves. He's a basket case. Hopefully, he will be better tomorrow, we need to finish making phone calls and arrangements. I will let you know about the arrangements, as soon as possible, so you can get a ticket to fly down for the funeral."

"Uhm, funeral," Mychal repeated. "I don't know if I can do it right now, Miracle. You know, I hate funerals."

"This is not just any funeral. This is family. I'm expecting you to be here." Mychal sighed under his breath.

"I heard that," she said. "I don't care what you say, you will be here. You didn't come to the wedding and I let you get away with it, but not again."

Miracle remembered six months ago, when she told Mychal that Joey was getting married in Atlanta and she wanted him to come with her. Mychal was on board and said he had cleared his calendar the weekend of the wedding and was going. Miracle was so happy for Joey and couldn't wait to be a part of his special day. She was going to be Joey's best women. Mark was in the wedding, as well. Miracle had purchased their tickets and had informed Rosita that she would need her while they went to Atlanta for Joseph's wedding. Everything was set and ready to go. The night before they were supposed to leave, Mychal came home from work with the bad news. He waited until they were in their bedroom alone.

"Miracle, I have something to tell you."

She looked at him puzzled. "What Mychal?"

"Uhm, Uhm. I'm not going to be able to go with you to the wedding."

"Mychal, why? You promised. We leave tomorrow. I have everything in place and ready to go."

"I know, baby. I know. Unfortunately, the big deal we were working on is about to fall through and Dave is freaking out. He wants me to close the deal and we really need to keep this contract, baby. It's worth millions. Believe me, I want to be there."

He was lying. He really didn't want to go in the first place, but he was going just to make her happy.

Miracle shot him a look. "For real, babe?"

"I'm not kidding. I can get Dave on the line right now, if you want," he said.

He knew she would never have him call anyone to verify his work. She didn't want to look crazy, nor have people think she doubted her husband.

"I will try my best to make the wedding," he lied. "The meeting is scheduled for early morning and the wedding is in the evening. Once the meeting is over I can hop on a flight and I should be able to make the wedding, or at least the reception."

Miracle knew Mychal was blowing smoke. He loved his job way too much. He would get wrapped up in stuff and could go for hours. She already knew she wouldn't see Mychal until she returned home from Atlanta. She was furious, but as always, she held it in and told him it was okay, when in reality, it wasn't. But what was she going to do? She didn't feel like arguing with him. She wanted to be excited and happy for Joseph. And not arrive upset and distracted, because of her own martial issues. She was going to a wedding. She didn't want to give off a bad marriage aura to a new couple, who was just getting married. It wouldn't be cool.

"Okay, Mychal. I really hope you can make it." She smiled reluctantly.

Miracle went to Atlanta the next day to stand by her brother on one of the most important days of his life, and her husband wasn't going to be there to support her. She was a little deflated and embarrassed.

And this too shall pass, Miracle thought as she smiled and stood by Joey's side.

The wedding went off without a hitch and was beautiful. It was Mychal's loss, since he didn't get to witness it.

"Do you have an idea when the funeral will be?" Mychal's question snapped her back.

"Probably, next week, I would guess. I'm going to fly back home, before the funeral, I believe and then we can fly back together. I can't stay here until next week. I need to get back and help Jen out with something for work. Let's just give it one more day to see how things go here, then, I can tell you better—once Joseph has made some calls and Tracey's parents arrive. Just be prepared. Plan on leaving your schedule open for early next week."

"Okay, Miracle. I will," Mychal responded.

"Mychal, I mean it. You aren't getting out of it this time. Please, don't make me pull out my old tricks." She laughed. "I know exactly what to do to get your butt to Atlanta. You know, I do. Try me, if you want to. I got to go."

She hung up before he could say another word.

He wouldn't get out of it this time. No way. She would pull his trump card for sure this time. Mychal knew for a fact, if he tried her, he would surely lose.

It was time Mychal knew the truth. Miracle was tired of keeping this secret.

Chapter Eleven

Karma

"Mrs. Wright, we got the results back from the test I ordered, and not much has changed. I was hoping the new treatment we started would give us some hope, or at least, a little improvement. I contacted an old friend, a colleague, and he is coming in from Denver, tomorrow. He has been doing some research and has been working on a few cocktails that have made progress on a couple of his patients in the Denver area. If you are willing to try it, we can. I will leave it totally up to you, because I know that you have been through a lot already. You're strong. I must say, most of my patients tend to give up long before the fight gets going. He will be here tomorrow, since he has other business in the area, as well. I told him about your case and he is willing to come by and meet with us. He may find something that we missed. This may be the answer we've been searching for or best, it could slow it down. Take the evening to think it over," the doctor explained.

Karma was listening intently, but she was tired. She was getting tired of trying. At some point, you just get tired of being tired and she was at that point.

"Okay, doc, let me sleep on it and pray to God for guidance. I must tell you, if I decide to do this, it will be the last one. If it doesn't work, please, promise me not to inform me of any other cocktails. I want to go home and spend what time I have left in my house surrounded by family. I refuse to spend my last days in a hospital around strangers, who know my condition, but don't know me as a person. I want to be with the people I love. Can you make the promise to me?" Karma asked.

She was serious as a heart attack.

The doctor knew she meant it. He grabbed her hand. "Yes, Karma, I promise this will be the last cocktail. If there is no change, I will arrange it so you can go home. We will make it as comfortable for you at home, as possible. They usually have a nurse come out once a day to administer medicine and to check on you. If your family is willing to do what is required to have you in hospice care at home, I have no problem with it at all. Just keep in mind, it can be a lot of work and sometimes cause strain on families. Please, make sure your family is ready to take on this responsibility. I will be monitoring your condition closely, at home. If things take a turn for the worst, please, consider returning. I know you probably won't, but the offer is on the table. Okay, I'm off my soapbox, now. Let us just concentrate on one thing at a time. I'm going to think optimistically. Let's pray, this cocktail my colleague has will be the one."

"Only God knows." Karma laughed.

The doctor smiled too. "Try to get some rest, Karma. I'll see you tomorrow," he said.

"Okay, see you, tomorrow," Karma replied. Karma sat there just thinking, *why me*?

Then she heard her grandma's voice, "Why not?" Those were her grandma's favorite words. Her grandma would always say, "God makes it rain on the just and unjust. Ain't nobody exempted. We just have to deal with it."

She never knew what her grandma was talking about, until she got older. But now she understood. She tried her best never to question God, but every so often she did.

"I hear you, grandma, but I'm still human and every once in a while, you still want answers. I never smoked a day in my life. Well, except for one time," she laughed.

She remembered it, just like it was yesterday. Her grandfather smoked a pipe and cigars. One day, they were all sitting outside on the porch and her grandfather lit his pipe. The smell of baked apples waffled into Karma's nostrils. It smelled so good, so she figured it had to taste just as good. She got up the courage to ask her grandpa, if she could smoke his pipe.

"Grandpa, can I taste the apples coming from your pipe?" Karma asked. Everyone got quiet and all eyes shifted to the man and the little girl. What was he going to do? She was clearly too young to smoke a pipe, but he figured, if she does it now, it will teach her a lesson. It was the way old folks thought, back then.

Karma's grandpa looked at his wife. He waited to see what she said. "Go on, let the crazy little thing have it," her grandma smirked.

She already knew what was going to happen. After this experience, she thought Karma would never smoke another day of her life and she was right.

Karma's grandpa shrugged his shoulders and handed her the pipe. He tried to give her instructions on what to do, but her grandma shook her head and he got quiet. She'll figure it out. Karma reached for the pipe and thought she was big time now. The wooden pipe was warm and felt good in between her small fingers. It was hand carved with intricate lines, and there was a name and date etched on one side, as well.

Karma inhaled deep and almost passed out. The smoke hit her lungs like a ton of bricks. Her eyes watered immediately and she began choking profusely. She almost peed on herself from choking and coughing. Her grandparents busted into laughter—simultaneously. Karma threw the pipe down to the ground.

"Whoa now, girl," her grandpa said. "That's my trusty pipe. You can't be throwing it down, you will crack it," he stated.

"Bet you won't want to smoke nothing else," her grandma chuckled. "Some things you just have to learn for yourself," she smirked. "If we would have told you what would happen you would not have believed us and you would've been curious about smoking until you tried it. See, now this way, you have it out of your system. Now, don't you?" she asked.

"I sure do," Karma managed to get out, while still choking. She thought she was going to die, right then and there.

Finally, here grandma got up and went inside the house and came back with a glass of water and gave it to Karma.

"Drink some of this water, before you choke to death," she snickered.

Karma knew from this day forward, she would never smoke a day in her life and she never did.

I don't understand it, Lord. I vowed from that day and I held up my end of the bargain. Why am I here facing lung cancer? Why?

Karma began to get angry. *I followed all the rules. I didn't smoke. I treated people right. I went to church. I paid my tithes. I helped others. I raised my children with respect. I never cheated… I, I, I.*

Karma was whimpering softly. She had a million thoughts running through her mind. She usually held it together, but at times it got to be too much, even for her to handle. She tried to put on the survivor role, especially in front of her children, but when she was alone with her thoughts—it got difficult, because the devil could always slip in.

She didn't wish this pain or ordeal on her worse enemy. No one should have to deal with this living hell.

We all have our cross to bear, she thought *and this one is mine*.

She had so many crosses thrown at her—all at once—and she didn't even do anything to cause this cross, well, not directly, she had to admit. She guessed maybe if she had made another decision, she may not be dealing with lung cancer, or the other foolishness.

Man, if she could just go back to the past. She should've known, he was trouble from the beginning. She vowed she would never smoke, but she never vowed she wouldn't be with someone who didn't smoke; and that's where the problem began.

Karma had no clue like most people.

How could she be so stupid? She thought.

Karma hated everything her husband stood for. But she also felt sorry for him and still prayed for him daily, because it's what she was supposed to do.

It was a struggle, but she was slowly coming to grips with what he had done and all the pain he had inflicted upon her. It was overwhelming. She joked with the Lord because she knew, she definitely had a seat on the right hand of God for the numerous times she'd been slapped by her husband and she'd turned the other cheek. It takes a special type of person to continually take abuse and pain; and never seek revenge.

"Lord, where is my reward? Will I see it here on earth, or once I make it to the pearly gates?"

Karma was trying to lighten her mood. She knew, if she continued down this road, it would only lead to hate and anger; and she really was trying to avoid those emotions and concentrate on the time she had left. She wanted to remain uplifted and appreciative of each day Jesus afforded her.

However, the human side will step in from time-to-time and remind us how those other emotions do exist. The human brain only weighs about 3 pounds, but once it gets to churning, it can feel like a ton.

Karma knew she was getting too deep in her own thoughts. She needed someone to talk to. She needed to hear her thoughts out loud. She knew exactly who she needed to speak to...

Karma picked up her cell phone.

"Hello," Miracle answered.

"Miracle," Karma murmured.

"Karma, what's wrong? What's going on? I can hardly hear you."

Miracle's heart started beating fast; she was getting scared. She was afraid of what Karma's answer might be.

"Miracle," Karma finally interjected. "I'm okay. I just needed someone to talk to and of course, I called you. Are you busy?" Karma asked.

Karma paused and added, "I'm sorry. I didn't even ask.

You are probably doing a million and one things, right now and don't have time to talk."

"Don't be silly!" Miracle said. However, she didn't know how good of a listener she was going to be right now. But this is what she does.

Dr. Miracle, she thought to herself.

She should've become a psychologist for real. Everyone calls her to get advice.

She fixes everyone else's problems, but who helps her deal with her own issues, she wondered.

This is how she felt, but she held it inside and never complained about it, at least, not to the people who called her for advice.

"What did Walter do, now?" Miracle asked. "Is he still seeing the same women?"

"Girl, I'm sure he is," Karma said holding back tears. "But I'm calling about another matter."

"What is it Karma? You're really scaring me. Tell me what's going on. If it's not Walter, is it the kids?"

"No," Karma said speaking softly again. "I'm in the hospital. Remember, a while back, I told you I wasn't feeling well. I thought I was a little under the weather with a cold or flu. I blew it off and took some medicine and kept going, because I was trying to deal with the crap with Walter. Well, I went to the doctor, because I just felt worse and couldn't get rid of the cough and I started coughing up blood."

"Blood," Miracle gasped.

"Yes, Miracle, please, let me say it. They ran test after test and found out that I have lung cancer."

"What… lung cancer? But you don't smoke," Miracle added.

"I know. I found out that you can get lung cancer from second-hand smoke. You don't have to be a smoker, but if you are around a smoker, you can still get it."

"What?" Miracle exclaimed. "That's crazy."

"Tell me about it," Karma responded.

Miracle thought for a second and then gasped again. "No, Karma. Say it ain't so? Walter? You got it from Walter?" Karma just started crying silently.

Miracle's heart sank. *How in the world could this poor woman have to deal with this too? Wasn't it bad enough she found out her husband was cheating? Now, he had given her lung cancer, as well. Damn.* Miracle thought.

Miracle didn't know what to say. She was going to lose it herself. First, Joey now this with Karma, she needed some wine.

It's not about you, Miracle.

"Karma," Miracle said softly. "Where is Walter, now?"

"I don't know," she responded. "Girl, he left, as soon as he found out I had lung cancer. He couldn't deal with it and he was out of there."

"Excuse me?" Miracle was trying to stay calm. "He left? Are you freaking kidding me? He left. I'm calling Mychal."

"Miracle, please, no!" Karma pleaded.

Karma wiped her face and begged Miracle. "Please, don't tell Mychal. He will kill Walter. I don't want it on my hands. You know Mychal never really liked him anyway. Walter isn't worth it."

"Karma, you need someone there with you."

"Why can't you come?" she asked.

"I'm in Atlanta." Miracle really didn't want to tell Karma what was going on with Joseph. She had enough to deal with right now. Lord knows, she didn't need to hear about death.

"Atlanta," Karma said.

"Yeah. I, I had to come take care of something with Joey." Miracle was a terrible liar. "I'm calling, Mychal."

"No, Miracle. I can't deal with Mychal, right now. Please, don't tell him."

"Karma, I will agree to it for right now, but I can't continue to keep secrets."

She was saying this more for herself, because the list of secrets was steadily growing. I already haven't told him about Walter cheating on you. He's going to be upset, when he finds out I knew."

"I know, Miracle, but you know how he is and I'm trying to relax and stay calm for the children. I have been praying and asking God for strength. I was doing well, but today, I just broke down."

"Well, hell, it's understandable," Miracle declared. "Oh, Karma. I wish I could be there. I will be back shortly and as soon as I get back, I will be headed to see you. I can't believe him. Then again, yes, I can. This is just like his stubborn behind. Oooh, I'm so upset. Sorry. Sorry. I'm sure you are past upset," Miracle fumed.

"Miracle, like I said I have been trying my best to stay prayed up and focused on God. I just hate it for my children. It is my only concern right now. It hurts me when I think of leaving them behind." She whimpered again, but didn't start crying.

"Karma, you know whatever I can do, I am here for you."

"I know. I know," Karma responded. "Since you are in Atlanta, we'll talk when you get back. I'm doing better. I just needed to talk it through and say it out loud."

"Are you sure you don't want me to call Mychal? I don't think you should be there alone."

"No, Miracle, I'm fine."

"When I get back, we are telling him what's going on. He's your brother and he has a right to know."

"Okay, okay, but not now. He will come over here and make matters worse."

"Yes, you're probably right," Miracle laughed.

"I know, I'm right," Karma replied.

"I'm not tall enough to whip Walter's butt and hurt him; however, I can break both of his legs, if necessary," Miracle said trying to lighten things up a bit.

They both laughed.

"Where are the kids?" Miracle asked.

"They're at home. My next door neighbor, Ms. Mable, is staying over. She came there, so the kids wouldn't have to disturb their routine. You know, her husband died last year, so she lives alone. She has been a lifesaver. Thank God for her."

"What are the doctors saying? When are you going home?"

"Well, they've tried a couple of different cocktails, to try and slow it down, but nothing has worked. There's a doctor from Denver coming and my doctor is hoping this new cocktail he has been working on will work or at least slow it down. Of course, there is no cure, but there is always hope. I told him, if this doesn't work, I want to go home. I don't want to spend what time I have left in a hospital. I want to be home with my children. I want to spend as much time with them, as possible. So, we will see. Miracle, I have talked your ear off long enough. I know you have to handle some stuff with Joseph. You said you were in Atlanta and I'm sure, it's for a reason."

"You let me worry about it," Miracle told her. "I can listen for as long as you need to talk. Joseph is napping right now, anyway."

"Well, someone just walked in my room anyway," Karma said. "I will talk to you when you get back."

"Who is it?" Miracle asked.

"Okay, mother Miracle," Karma teased.

Miracle could hear a voice in the background, but couldn't make it out or what they were saying.

"Bye, Miracle," Karma said. "Call me when you return. I'll be fine. Tell Joseph, hello."

Karma hung up the phone before Miracle could say another word. Miracle looked at the phone. "Oh, no, she didn't hang up on me."

Miracle wondered who had entered the hospital room. She couldn't wait to get back to see her sister-in-law.

Geez… What was next?

Chapter Twelve

Karma

Walter walked into the hospital room with one intention on his mind. He didn't care if she was sick. It had nothing to do with him. He was moving on with his life. He didn't have time for a sick wife. He had already found him a new boo and she was da bomb and she wasn't sick. They had been dating for about six months. She was there for him for what he was going through.

No one saw his side. It was tough trying to care for sick people. He had seen it before and vowed he would never go through it—again. It didn't matter who it was. He wasn't going to do it. It was bad Karma got sick, but she would have to figure it out on her own. He wasn't sick and hardly ever got sick. He was as healthy as a horse. He wouldn't get tied down with sickness. He still had the best years of his life ahead of him.

"What the hell are you doing here?" Karma asked.

"Hello to you to," he retorted.

"You have a lot of nerve showing up here. What did you come to see, if I was dead, yet?" Karma shot at him.

He was slow to answer and just stared at her for a minute.

"Karma, I didn't come here to argue with you. I'm sorry that you are sick, whether you believe it, or not."

"Oh, really! You sure have a funny way of showing it. Why are you here, Walter? You want something. I know that's the only reason why you are here. I don believe you came here to make small talk and see how I am doing. So, just spit it out."

"Karma, don't be like that."

"Like what? Are you serious, right now? I'm the one lying here sick with lung cancer. I never smoked a day in my life, but you smoked a pack, sometimes two a day. I found out my husband is cheating on me with one of my friends, I won't see my children become adults, get married or my grandkids and you have the nerve to tell me, don't be like that. Man, you have some nerve. You must think your balls are the size of an elephant. Trust me they aren't big at all. I was married to you for twenty years. I know them very well. Walter, what is it? Why are you here?"

Walter did feel a bit of remorse for all he had done, but he didn't know how to express it; so, he did what he did best, be an ass. He was raised knowing men don't show weakness. A real man is strong and hard. Nothing breaks him down.

His father would say, "Son, never let anyone see you vulnerable. If so, you will be considered a punk. Men are supposed to be tough, strong, and invincible."

His dad talked all kinds of junk and never let Walter express any emotion and would whip him, if he cried.

However, things changed quickly, when Walter's mom got sick with cancer and his dad had to take care of her. Walter's dad fell apart. For the first time, he saw his father cry. It was the most horrifying sound Walter had ever heard in his life. He didn't know what to do. He had never seen his dad like this. The man who was always so super strong was now weak as a wet noodle. He had no clue what to do.

He thought he was always the strong one, but it was Walter's mother. He would never admit it, but it was true. Still, 'till this day, he will say that he was the hammer in the family. When he saw him fall to his knees, he knew the truth.

He watched his dad deteriorate right in front of his eyes, as he cared for his mother. He vowed, back then, he would never go through sickness in his life—with no one.

He thought he was in the home stretch with Karma. They had been married for twenty years and both had been healthy, until now. He just couldn't do it.

He wasn't going to end up like his dad. Oh, Hell No!

Karma cleared her throat.

"Well. I just need you to sign these papers," Walter stumbled.

He reached into his jacket pocket and pulled out some papers. He handed them to Karma.

"Sign what papers, Walter? I know you have not come into this hospital with divorce papers and expect me to sign them. Are you high? You must be high on something. I didn't think you got high, since you were a teenager. But you must be high."

"Karma, now, you know I'm not high. I haven't smoked since we were kids."

"Oh, no, you've smoked," she yelled.

"Calm down, Karma. You know what I mean. I haven't smoked any weed."

"It doesn't have to be weed. Shoot, all this new stuff out, now. You can pretty much smoke anything, nowadays."

"Karma, I haven't smoked any drugs. Please, stop. I don't need anyone hearing you say that. I don't want rumors spreading and getting to my job. They do periodic drug testing. All I need is to be called in because they suspect I'm using drugs. It's hard enough for a good black man to get a job."

Karma laughed. "Good black man, huh. I don't think good men cheat on their wives, while they are ill and then, leave them. It seems like a weak man to me," she uttered.

"Karma, I didn't come here to do this with you," he sighed. "We should act like adults and be civil toward one another. I just want to move on with my life. I don't want anything from you, other than your signature and a few things. I'm not trying to make this difficult."

He was really trying to act like he cared and it pissed Karma off, even more. He was being so condescending. Karma wished she had the strength and energy to climb out of bed and whip his ass. Maybe she should have let Miracle call Mychal. He would have been here when Walter came and all hell would have broken loose. This clown, and he was a clown, needed his ass whipped.

Lord, help me, please, Karma pleaded to herself.

She was starting to revert to her old ways and it wouldn't be long before she did or said something, she really would regret.

I can't stoop way down to his level. Reel it back, sista girl. He's baiting you with this calm, cool attitude. You know this man. You have to play the fiddle, not the fool.

Karma took a deep breath and smiled.

"You're right, Walter. We need to be civil. We are adults and we should be civil. Leave the papers here with me, and I will look at them later. I don't sign anything without reviewing it, first. Please, give me a couple of days and I will get back with you, once I've had a chance to look them over."

Walter smiled broadly. "Now, that's my girl. I knew you would come around and see things my way," he said.

He tried to touch Karma's hand, but she moved it quickly.

"Okay, okay," he said. "I apologize. I just wanted to kiss your hand and show you I do still care about you, Karma."

"Walter, I think it's time for you to go. I will call you in a few days. Leave the papers over there on the table."

Karma turned over and faced the window. Her back was to Walter and she said nothing further.

Walter got the message. He dropped the papers on the small hospital table and took one last look at Karma's backside and walked out the room.

Karma was looking out the window thinking. *This can't be real. After giving this man twenty years of my life, this is how he treats me. Walter Wright "karma" is a bad thing. SHE ALWAYS WINS IN THE END!*

Karma smiled and closed her eyes.

Chapter Thirteen

Patrick

The house was silent. The kids were in their rooms. Mychal was in the media room watching ESPN.

Patrick had descended the stairs talking to himself about the good, old days…

"I can't believe, I found you after all these years."

His mind was playing tricks on him. He was confused. He was just talking to Miriam.

Where did she go? She was just here and we were talking. How did you disappear so fast?

Patrick had to get out of there and find her now. He reached the door and unlocked it and twisted the knob.

The deafening sound of the alarm shocked Mychal. Mychal grabbed a slugger bat from the corner and headed out of the media room. He was ready to knock the block off somebody's head. He creeped around the corner and caught a glimpse of Patrick headed out of the front door.

What the hell? Mychal thought to himself. *Where is he going this time of night? Patrick never leaves the house this late.*

Mychal ran over and turned off the alarm. He called out to Patrick, but he was out of the door. Mychal followed him outside.

"Patrick, where are you going?"

Patrick was walking down the street talking to himself.

Where's he going? He thought.

Mychal started a light jog to catch Patrick. He was moving fast. He reached Patrick at the corner.

"Dad, where are you going?"

Patrick turned around and looked at Mychal like he had never seen him a day in his life. His eyes were distant. He was a million miles away. Mychal didn't know what to do. He had never seen Patrick like this before. Miracle told him Patrick had done a couple of strange things, but he was never around to see it.

Of course, he ran out of the house and forgot his cell phone. He needed, Miracle. He had no clue what to do.

The two men just stood there looking at each other.

Mychal saw the lights. The police pulled into the block. With lights flashing, the police exited the vehicles with their hands on their guns, but they weren't drawn.

"What's going on here?" One of the officers yelled.

Mychal raised his hands and said, "This is my father-in-law. He just left the house and set off the alarm. I followed him out here and now, he's acting weird," Mychal stated with his hands still raised.

He didn't want any trouble. He knew about all the recent police shootings of black men and he surely didn't want to become a statistic.

"Oh, so it's your alarm that went off. We were responding to the call. We were sent to check it out and make sure everything was ok. The house is fine, but I don't know if everything is okay," Mychal replied.

"What's going on?" the officer asked.

"I don't know."

He was trying not to panic. It wouldn't do any good and would probably freak out Patrick even more.

"We were in the house and the next thing I know, I hear the alarm going off. I thought someone had broken in. I was watching television. I came out of the media room to see my father-in-law walking out of the front door. I called his name, but he just kept on going, like he didn't hear me at all. I've never seen him like this." Mychal explained.

"Do you need an ambulance?" the officer asked.

"I don't know. I need my cell phone, so I can call my wife." The officer looked at Mychal funny.

Mychal quickly added, "This is her dad and she would know what to do."

"Oh, okay," the officer grinned.

"Where is your phone?" he asked.

"In the house, I ran out after him and left everything. Matter of fact, I need to get back, because I left the front door open. If I can just get him down the stree. We can figure everything out down there."

Patrick was looking around and staring from one person to another.

"Where is she?" Patrick finally blurted out. "Did y'all find her?"

The officer looked at Mychal.

Mychal shrugged his shoulders. "Find who?" he asked Patrick.

Patrick laughed. "Miriam," he stated as a matter of fact.

"Oh, okay," Mychal kind of understood, now.

"Dad, Miriam is at the house." Mychal lied.

He had to say something to get him back to the house. He didn't want anyone to walk into the house, besides the kids were still upstairs. They probably hadn't even budged. Sometimes, he thought they were deaf. If they had on their head phones, you could forget it.

"Dad, let's go back home. Miriam is at home. She's waiting for you."

Patrick still looked confused, but he asked, "She's home?"

A slight grin appeared on his face. Then it disappeared. "No, she's not there. I just left and she wasn't there. That's why I'm out here looking for her."

Mychal knew he had to remain calm.

"May I?" the officer said.

"Please, do," Mychal said.

The officer motioned for his female partner. The male

officer whispered something in her ear. The female officer started speaking in a low voice to Patrick.

"Come on, Patrick, we have to go meet Miriam at the house," she stated. Patrick looked at the female and his eyes lit up.

She reached out and took Patrick's hand. She began walking him slowly down the street to the house.

Mychal watched in amazement.

The officer was able to get Patrick down the street and into the house.

Mychal didn't know what he would have done, if the police hadn't showed up. He figured he probably would have been out there for a while arguing with Patrick, had they not come.

"Does everything look in order?" the male officer questioned.

Mychal replied, "Yes."

"We can do a walk through if you like."

Of course, Mychal declined. "No. We're good. I'm going to get him back to bed and pray that he doesn't get out. Thanks again for coming."

"No, problem, sir. Have a good night," the male officer replied.

"Good luck with your father-in-law," the female officer added.

Mychal was talking with the officers at the door when the house phone rang. He let it ring. He figured one of the children would get it. He knew they weren't sleep.

Just as he closed the door, Mason yelled downstairs, "Dad, get the phone. It's mom."

Mychal cringed a little. He really didn't want to talk to Miracle, right now. He was not a good liar and she could read right through him.

"Hey, babe," Mychal chimed in on the cordless phone. She didn't even speak for a second.

"Mychal, what is going on over there?"

"Huh?"

"Don't play games with me. I just got a call from the security system."

Damn, he was thinking. He forgot Miracle's cellphone was the contact number on file.

"The alarm company told me there was some kind of motion from the front door. Is everything okay? Did someone try to break in? They dispatched the police to check it out."

"Geez… can I answer a question?" Mychal interjected.

"Sorry," Miracle responded. She finally took a breath. "Everything is fine. It was dad."

"Dad," Miracle grimaced. Her heart started beating fast. "Is he alright?"

"Yes, he's fine. He just opened the door, after I had already put the alarm on. I couldn't get to it in enough time, before the police came out. They just left."

"You're not telling me everything," Miracle added.

"What are you talking about?" Mychal tried to stay cool.

She didn't play when it came to her family. Even though they drove her absolutely crazy, she protected them, at all cost. Miracle was like a tiger ready to attack.

Any sign of weakness and she would pounce for the kill, if someone messed with her family.

He tried to be short and to the point. He knew this wouldn't work with his wife.

She was going to want to know every detail.

"Mychal, I know you. You're lying. You might as well tell me what's going on. I will find out anyway. I always do," she smiled.

Damn this woman, Mychal thought.

He hated it, but he knew she was right. She was going to find out. It was like this damn woman had physic powers.

"Well, I'm waiting," Miracle stated.

"I was in the media room watching television when I heard the alarm go off. I came out to see dad walking out the front door. I called out to him, but he kept going. It was like he was a totally different person. He was confused and lost. It was like he was a kid. He wouldn't talk or respond at all. When the police arrived, he finally started coming around. He was talking about your mom and how he had to find her. I never saw him like this, Mir. It was so strange. It was his eyes. His eyes are what threw me. It was like he was miles away. He was here, but he wasn't here, if that makes sense. Miracle, he didn't even know it was me. I still don't think he's back, yet. His body is present, but his mind definitely is somewhere else. I was just about to get him back upstairs and try to get him in bed."

"I tried to tell you. Remember? You told me I was crazy. I told you something was going on with him."

I remember you saying, "Uhm, huh. You worry too much, Miracle. Ain't nothing wrong with him." Miracle mocked Mychal. She chuckled.

"Now you see for yourself. I'm calling the doctor as soon I get back. We need to get to the bottom of this. He just zones out. He eventually comes back."

"Let me get him upstairs and I'll call you back," Mychal warned.

"Ok, but call me back. If not, I'll be calling you."

"I know. I know," Mychal laughed.

Chapter Fourteen

Miracle

Miracle hung up the phone. She really was on the verge of a break down. It was like an avalanche was chasing her and she was running downhill, but wasn't moving fast enough. She was about to be buried alive. It was one thing, after another.

Miracle wasn't a drinker, but right now, she needed a stiff one—a drink. She laughed to herself. The other stiff one probably wouldn't hurt either.

Between, Joey, Karma and her dad, she was going to be crazy her damn self. This was getting old quick.

She tried to tell Mychal. He thought she was crazy. She noticed it a while ago. It was just little things. Her dad couldn't remember where he put his car keys. He would be cooking something and forget he had the pot on the burner. You would ask him a question and he would act as if he was going to answer, then just stare into space. It came and went. He didn't do it all the time. It was infrequent, but enough to have him checked out.

Miracle thought she knew what was going on, but refused to say it. She thought if she didn't say or mention it or think about it, then it wouldn't be true. Not her dad. Not, the Patrick Jones. He couldn't be sick. He was one of the strongest men she knew.

Nothing could knock him down.

Miracle could feel herself about to lose it, but she held it back. She had to be strong for Joey. She couldn't break down—not now. She would have to wait until she got home.

Home, once she got home, she would have to be honest with Mychal. He was going to be pissed. She just got on him about lying to her and she's been doing the same thing. It wasn't going to be pretty.

She was going to find Mark. A drink was in order, then, she would help Joey finish up.

She needed to get her butt on a plane quick to deal with the rest of her family issues. Miracle would return to Atlanta for the funeral, but for now she needed to get home—before all hell broke loose with Karma and Dad.

Chapter Fifteen

Miracle

Miracle felt a little better the next morning, when she awoke. She had bent Mark's ear well into the wee hours of the morning, trying to talk through her dramas. Mark had always been a good listener and never judged. She understood why Joseph adored him, so much. He could listen and not interrupt. There's nothing worse, than when you're coming to someone with your problems, and before you know it, you're dealing with their issues.

When you get done, you still have no sound advice for your problems.

Miracle really didn't have anyone to express her drama with, so Mark was a much needed ear. Usually, she is the listener and drama fixer. They chatted over drinks, laughed, cried and laughed some more, and then went to bed. At least for a few hours, she was free from her worries.

"Joy always comes in the morning!" Mark told her. "We don't know when the morning will be here, but if we keep living, the morning will come."

Miracle smiled. She sighed. And the burden was lifted.

She had just a little more strength to make it, at least

through this day. She decided she would shower first and then cook breakfast for Joseph and Mark. They could use the time to finalize everything. Joseph had already received the green light from Tracey's parents to handle the service the way he saw fit. It wasn't difficult, because Tracey had left detailed instructions before dying. There was no doubt in his mind that Joseph would handle it as instructed, plus more.

Miracle was in the kitchen cooking and hymning, when Joseph walked in.

"Good morning, sunshine," Miracle smiled.

"Good morning," he replied.

"You're looking better this morning," she added.

"I feel a little better," he managed with a slight smile. "You know, Miracle, this has to be the most difficult thing I have ever done. I mean I have been through some crazy stuff and did some things, but this pain right here is unexplainable. I wouldn't wish it on anyone, not even my nemesis. It's like a piece of me has been cut off and I'm trying to find it, but it has disappeared. People keep telling me that they understand my pain, it will be okay, he's in a better place and so on and so on. I really don't want to hear it right now. I want to know how to make my heart stop hurting. How do I continue to live when part of me is dead? No one has answered that question, yet. They don't know how I feel. They couldn't because, if they did, they wouldn't say certain things."

Joey looked out the kitchen window and then added, "I get it. I do. I know people are only trying to comfort me, but sometimes the best things said are the words never spoken. That's what I love about you, Mir. You listen. You just comfort me and let me be me. I just want to take this time to say thank you. I know things have been crazy and will get crazier before the funeral is over, so please know that I love you and appreciate you always being there for me, no matter what. In all of this craziness, if I said it before, just know that I really mean it."

Joey was tearing up. "Okay, enough said," he admitted. "I will not cry. Not now. We have to make it through these arrangements, so I can truly begin my healing. Besides, I can only imagine what your household is like right now."

He chuckled, just thinking about it.

"I know, Mychal is playing the cocky role with his big ole chest on 'swole.' But believe me, he is losing it. Men kill me acting like they can handle it all when the wives are gone, but honey child, we know the truth. Behind every strong man is a stronger woman. Hello," Joseph chimed.

"I will definitely agree," Miracle laughed.

It was good to see Joey laugh, she thought.

She was praying hard for her brother. She couldn't imagine anyone having to bury their spouse. Despite the drama her and Mychal faced, she would be a basket case, if he suddenly passed away.

The thought sent a chill up her spine and she shuttered for a brief second.

She had become so accustomed to having him around. They had been together a long time. Just thinking about it… was a very awkward moment. When Miracle and Mychal met…

It was move-in day on campus. Cars, students, parents and stuff was everywhere. Miracle was so excited to be moving away from home. She had pretty much lived a sheltered life. Her parents were strict and didn't play. She felt like she was finally getting her wings. They were unloading the car and moving stuff into the dorm. The dorm was co-ed, which her father didn't like, but couldn't do anything about it.

"I don't like this one bit, Miriam," he said angrily.

"Patrick there is nothing we can do, right now. The girl will be fine. We have raised her properly. She knows right from wrong. Now, calm down and keep moving this stuff."

Patrick continued, but was fussing under his breathe. Miracle didn't even notice the tall, handsome young man, who was parked behind them. She just wanted her parents to hurry up, so she could enjoy her new-found freedom. Her dad was so busy fussing he didn't realize that the top to one of her bins was not completely closed. Miracle was trying to adjust the bin her dad had just given her, it fell and all of the contents spilled over into the street and onto the sidewalk.

Mychal was walking by at the same time when the bin tumbled from her hands. Of course, it was the bin with her personal hygiene items. Out rolls the bag of Kotex pads and tampons and landed right at Mychal's feet.

Miracle stood frozen for a few seconds and dropped her head. She was utterly embarrassed. Mychal bent down and she almost lost it, but she didn't say anything. He picked the items up and handed them back to Miracle.

"Uhm, uhm, thank you," was all she could manage to say. When she looked up and saw Mychal's face, she was still frozen.

This man was gorgeous. It made her even more embarrassed.

Great! She thought.

Of course, one of the best-looking men she had ever seen in her life picked up her unmentionables.

"No problem," Mychal responded smiling.

He had the whitest teeth she had ever seen. This man was a god. She could kill her dad.

"Hello, I'm Mychal," he said, as he extended his hand.

She was expecting his hands to be rough and dry, but was pleasantly surprised. His hands were as soft as cotton.

"And you are?" he asked.

"Oh, I'm sorry. I'm Miracle."

"Wow! Miracle, huh? Well, maybe this was divine intervention," he joked.

"Really!" Miracle laughed.

"You never know. Maybe?"

"Or just dumb luck," Miracle responded. She turned and looked at her dad, who was still fussing. He was fiddling with other bins in the car, oblivious of the rolling pads and tampons.

"I guess, only time will tell," Mychal smiled again.

"Thanks, again," Miracle said. "I'm truly sorry you had to pick those up," she said shyly.

"No worries," he said. "I have a mother and sister. It's no biggie. I'm used to them."

Miracle gave him a raised eyebrow. She couldn't believe this big hunk of a guy was saying he was used to tampons.

"Hold up! Hold up!" he said. "It's not like that."

"Like what?" Miracle grinned.

"I'm just saying, I know what they are and it's no big deal. I used to have to go pick them up sometimes from the store for my mom or my sister. That's all."

"Really," Miracle added.

"Yes, really," he stated as matter of fact. "I don't have a problem with it. Trust me, I'm very secure in my manhood," he said a little too cocky.

I bet you are, Miracle was thinking.

She blushed. He noticed her blush and smiled.

"Miracle," her dad called.

He had finally looked up and saw what was going on.

"Yes," she responded.

"I have to go," she added.

"Yeah, me too," he replied

"Nice meeting you, Miracle. If the powers to be have their way, I shall see you again my Miracle." He jogged away.

Miracle stood there for a minute following him with her eyes. He was confident and cocky. She liked it and hated it— at the same time. To say the least, she was intrigued. She hoped she would see him again.

The beep of the coffee maker snapped Miracle back to this morning. Joseph was still talking, but she hadn't heard anything he had said.

"Mir, you okay?" Joseph asked.

"Yes, I'm good. I was just listening and thinking of some of the good times we had. I will truly miss Tracey, as well. He was like another brother/sister I wish I had."

She laughed.

"What's so funny?" Mark asked as he walked into the kitchen.

"Just reminiscing about some good times with Tracey and trying to boost my spirit a bit."

"Good," Mark responded cheerfully.

"It smells wonderful in here," he added. "I can't believe you're up cooking this early. We just laid down a couple hours ago. I don't know where you get the energy," Mark said yawning.

"Trust me, the only reason I'm up is because I smelled bacon. Honey, I don't care how tired I am, when I smell bacon, I rise."

They laughed.

"You are just in time. The coffee just beeped and the bacon will be done in a few minutes. I have omelets coming up and there is fresh fruit on the tray. Dig in. You need to feed the alcohol. We're not as young as we used to be. I love you, but I won't be cleaning that up. Eat up!"

The funeral was set for a week away. They had finally gotten everything settled. Joseph and Tracey's parents were both happy with the arrangements. No expense was spared. Tracey's parents were going to stay in Atlanta until everything was over. It was no rush for them to get back home. It was just the two of them, so they could stay for as long as they wished. Their neighbor back home was keeping an eye on their house, so all was well.

Miracle had booked her return flight home for late in the evening. She was glad she could be here for Joseph, but she couldn't wait to see her family. She picked up her cell phone to call Mychal and let him know she would be home later this evening.

"Hello," he answered.

"Hey, babe. How's dad?"

"Back to his old self," Mychal said. "I don't even know, if he remembers what happened last night. He got up this morning and nonchalantly fell back into his regular routine. He didn't say anything, so neither did I. I figured, we would discuss it when you returned." he said.

"Speaking of returning I'll be back late tomorrow evening," Miracle said.

"Already?" Mychal responded.

"Don't sound so excited," Miracle broke in.

"I didn't mean it like that, babe. Did you guys get everything squared away?" Mychal clarified.

"We did. The funeral is next week. Joseph wanted to give everyone enough time to travel to Atlanta. Tracey has family and friends overseas, so Joey wanted to be considerate of them."

"That was nice." Mychal commented. "I guess Tracey was loved by many. I'm sorry I never met her," he added.

Miracle cleared her thought.

She wanted to tell him so bad—"she" was a "he"—but she knew how homophobic her husband was and she just couldn't do it—not now. Besides doing it over the phone was not appropriate, either. She had managed to keep the fact of Joseph being gay from Mychal all these years.

When they had gotten married, Joey wasn't out of the closet, yet; so, it was easy to keep it under wraps. Joseph had been between the states and overseas most of their marriage, so that helped, as well. The few times Joseph had come to visit, it was brief and he never came with any of his lovers. If they were with him on the trip, he wouldn't bring them around Miracle's family and she definitely didn't have to worry about her dad saying anything. Patrick was in complete denial.

Mychal kind of suspected it, but he really didn't want to know anyway. He wanted nothing to do with gay men. He never asked and Miracle never volunteered the information. Some things are just better untouched and this was one of them. However, it had come time for her to not only touch the subject, but to get Mychal and her dad to agree to attend the funeral and face the fact. She didn't know what she was going to do. Hopefully, her born name would reign true and maybe by some divine power, she could pull off a "Miracle" with these two. This was one subject, Patrick and Mychal, both totally agreed upon—no questions asked.

She was going to have to dig deep into her bag of tricks for this one.

Lord, only you, she was thinking. *My name is Miracle and I need one.*

"Okay sweetie, I got to go," she said. "I need to pack and Joey and I have some last-minute errands, before I leave for the airport.

Miracle had to get off the phone. She didn't want to take the chance of slipping up and saying the wrong thing.

"Make sure you talk to Aaron and let him know that you have to come to Atlanta next week for a funeral." She added.

"I don't want any excuses this time. You didn't make the wedding, so you must come to the funeral."

Miracle didn't know why she was pushing this so hard. If Mychal didn't come, he would never have to find out Tracey was a "he." It was like his coming was her way of freeing herself from the lie all of these years. She knew it was going to cause drama, but for some reason she felt, he had to know. She was a bit chicken to come out and say it and she would have felt like a true coward, if she told him after the fact. The next couple of days were going to be a true test for her marriage.

Was it as strong as she thought? Only time would tell.

Chapter Sixteen

Mychal

Mychal really didn't want to attend the funeral, but he knew, if he wanted to keep peace in his home, he would not have a choice. He didn't want to talk to Aaron. He didn't care too much for Aaron and thought he should have Aaron's job anyway. Aaron was only in the position because John, the CEO, was his dad. Mychal had been there longer and knew more. When Aaron graduated from college, of course, he got the position Mychal had been working his butt off to earn. The "good ole boy" network was in full effect. The funny thing was that John really didn't want Aaron in the position either, but his hands were tied. John was the CEO, but his wife's family owned the company. The wife wore the pants and it was no way her son was going to play second fiddle to some black man, who used to be a basketball player. There was no way he knew more than her Aaron.

Huh, he laughed. *This ball player could run hoops around Aaron on the court and in the board room. Ball playing had afforded me a very good education. I'm ten times smarter than Aaron, but my skin is the wrong color,* he thought.

Aaron barely graduated. He had been privileged all his life

and never had to work hard for anything. It was completely opposite for Mychal. He earned everything he had through hard work. His dad made sure of it. Mychal had a slight distaste for white boys, since his encounter in college. He was cordial towards them, but hated the entitled arrogance he thought they portrayed. He was no extremist with his disdain, but he wasn't inviting white folks to his house for dinner, either. There was no way around it. He would have to suck it up and tell Aaron he had to go out of town. He knew Aaron would have something smart to say. It would take all his cool points to keep from chopping Aaron in his throat. He would go to John, but he was on vacation, this week.

Usually, Mychal bypassed Aaron and spoke directly to John when he needed something. He and John had an understanding relationship. It didn't hurt that Mychal had a little dirt on John, as well, but they had an agreement. Mychal was holding up his end of the deal, but John would have to pay up, soon.

Mychal decided he would go for a run to relax his mind. He threw on some running gear and was out the door.

It would be interesting to finally see Joseph's spouse, he thought, just as he hit his stride.

It was sad it took death for him to meet her, but he always thought Joseph was gay. Maybe he was wrong. He just knew he was, though. He was usually right, but he guessed for once, he was off.

"I guess it could happen, once," he said out loud and a smile spread across his face.

It was just strange though that Miracle never talked about Joseph's wife. Why was it such a secret? Mychal realized he never mentioned it either, so maybe Miracle just was too busy trying to keep the family on track. Goodness knows, we're all over the place. They were always busy with all of the extra-curricular activities for the kids. Well, maybe he should re-think it: Miracle was always busy. Mychal played a part. It was a small part. but he did play a part. He realized it and at times he tried, but it was hard for him. To be honest, he really didn't know how, but he was too ashamed to ask. Now, when it came to working outside the house and providing for his family, he couldn't be touched. He just had a hard time translating it into the household like most men, not all but the majority.

Mychal was headed back home and the run had him feeling better already. His wife would be home this evening and he could love on her and release some frustration. He enjoyed making love to Miracle—after all of these years.

She still could get the best rise out of him. She had played the sweet innocent role, when they met, but she was really a freak. He didn't know where she got it from, but she turned into someone different in the bedroom. She had skills and he loved it. He had been with plenty of women, over the years due to his career, but it was Miracle, who stole his heart and libido. No other woman got him as excited and erect, as she did. She could walk in the room and move a certain way and he was hard as a brick wall. There were no inhibitions with her and he cherished it. Most men only dreamed of having those emotions with their wife. He had only experienced that feeling one other time.

Whoa! Where did that thought come from?

He had suppressed the incident way down in his skeleton closet and had thrown away the key many moons ago. He vowed he would never speak or think of it—again. He had experienced an orgasm, so powerful that it scared him. Mychal was drunk when it happened, but he remembered the orgasm.

Why was he thinking of this now? It had been a very long time. No one else, but Miracle had come close to giving him that feeling, so he knows it is part of the reason he married her. Sex is a powerful thing. Sexual tension can make you do things you never dreamed you would ever do. It can take you to a dark place and suck you in, if you're not careful.

Mychal turned up his music to drown out his thoughts. He was trying to wash the memory from his mind. He wasn't sure what triggered it, but he damn sure would control it. His manhood was starting to tingle and he was fighting hard to hold back.

I need to focus. Focus, damn it.

The swaying trees and hard beat of the concrete wasn't helping, because it reminded him of the pounding and thumping of that night. He was starting to get a serious erection.

"Damn it," he said again.

Think. Think. He got it. His thoughts lead him to "Butt Ugly" at the restaurant.

His penis immediately went limp. He thought of her gold teeth around his manhood and the thrill was immediately gone.

"Whew... thank you, Butt Ugly," he hissed.

He knew she would come in handy for something one day. And this was the day.

Mychal finished up his run and his thoughts were clear. He had to figure out how to erase "that" night from his mind, if not, it would be hell to pay. His life, as he knew it, would be shaken. Hell, it would be over. He would lose everything.

Miracle could never, ever find out about "that" night. NEVER!

Chapter Seventeen

Patrick

Patrick and the kids were in the kitchen having breakfast, when Mychal walked in from his run.

"Kind of late this morning, aren't you, dad?" McKenzie asked.

"Are you going to work, today?" Mason asked.

"Yes, to both of you," he answered. "I'm a little late, because I decided to run at the last minute. I needed to clear my head," he confessed. "Running is good for the mind and soul."

"If you say so," McKenzie sighed.

She hated running. It made her sweat too much. She wanted nothing to do with a lot of sweat. She danced, but it was different, because she enjoyed dancing, so the sweat didn't bother her. Dancing was the only time she didn't mind sweating.

"I'm going in a little later," he directed himself toward Mason, now. "I had a conference call early this morning with an overseas client, due to the time change, so I'm going in a little late, since I had to get up early. I talked to mom this morning, also. She'll be home this evening."

Patrick squirmed a little in his seat. He wasn't ready to face Miracle.

He knew Mychal told her what happened last night. See, it was a man code for the two of them, not to bring it up. It was just understood.

But now, it wasn't going to be so easy with Miracle. She would have a million and one questions. Unfortunately, he didn't have the answers, either. He had no damn clue what the hell was going on. He just knew he didn't like it. One minute, he was talking to his sweet Miriam, laughing and joking, then, the next, he was outside in his pajamas with the police.

Miriam was gone and he felt lost. He had no explanation. No one wants to figure it out more than him. He might as well get prepared, because it was coming whether he wanted it or not. It felt like the roles were reversing. He would have to remind her that he was still her father. He missed his Miriam, so much.

Why did his precious jewel have to be snatched away, so soon?

Patrick remembered when he found Miriam.

After he found Miriam in Woolworth's all those years ago, he knew destiny had bought them back together. He visited her every day. They talked and laughed; and he sat there for hours just watching her.

Finally, on the fifth of June he decided it was time. The soda pop he drank had cost him five cents. She was supposed to get married in five days. Five was his favorite number. It was triple fives, so he figured it was now or never. He felt lucky. The bus number that he rode on to Philadelphia was 555. Everything was lined up. It had to be destiny.

"Miriam, I know this may sound crazy," he said as he walked her home "But I love you and have loved you from the first time I saw you. I know my timing sucks and you are getting married in five days, but I know, if you marry him it will be a big mistake. I promise, I will take care of you and you will never want for anything."

"Patr…" he cut her off.

"No, please, hear me out. I have to get it all out," he insisted.

He sighed. "This isn't no little kid crush. I can't explain it. I just know. It took me all these years to find you and I won't lose you again. Now, I know I'm asking a lot of you. I leave for Camp Lejeune soon and I want to know that when I get back you will be my wife. Hell, we can get married before I leave. I am serious. I want, I mean I need you, Miriam."

Miriam was speechless. She didn't know what to say. She finally pointed out, "Patrick, I'm getting married in five days. I mean, I've enjoyed seeing you and spending time with you, but my wedding is already planned. How will I explain it to my parents and his parents, the guests and the Pastor? Do you know how it would look?"

"I don't give a shit how it looks," Patrick expressed. "I care about you and me. Nothing else matters. I'm about to serve my country and the only other thing I care about right now is knowing you will have me as your husband."

"Patrick, this is so much, so soon. I don't know what to say. You must understand, I need some time. I mean, I care about you, I do. No one makes me laugh like you do and you are the only person I know who can stomach Woolworth's food so many days in a row," she smiled.

"I really can't," Patrick admitted "But I did it, just to be close to you. Don't you see, Miriam? Do you really think I want to eat that mess every day? I would prefer to have a home cooked meal, especially, if my wife prepared it," he grinned.

Miriam looked away And then added, "Patrick, I need time. Please, don't expect me to answer you right now. I don't think you would like the answer. I have to absorb all of this. Give me a couple of days to figure this out. Please."

They reached Miriam's house and she kissed Patrick on the cheek and walked inside and closed the door.

Patrick went back to F. W. Woolworth Company every day after that night, and Miriam was nowhere to be found.

She had confided in her mother about what happened with Patrick and asked her mother to please not tell her father, but of course, her mother told her father. Her father made her quit her job and told her she could never see Patrick again. Miriam was crushed.

Her father explained how Patrick was a fool and he only wanted to marry her because he was afraid he would not come back from the war. He wanted something to latch onto and it was her.

"You're a fool, if you think for one minute that he cares about you. He's going off to the military and will meet all kinds of women. You'll be back here waiting on him and he'll be whoring around with women from different countries. Not my daughter. I won't allow it," her father had proclaimed.

Miriam was heart-broken.

She couldn't believe her mother had betrayed her. She thought her mother, of all people, would understand, since she had been forced to marry someone other than her true love. Her mother had never forgiven her grandmother.

Her father refused to let her see or talk to Patrick. He told her she was to be married in five days and that was the end of it.

Patrick was crushed. He left for Camp Lejeune broken, but not defeated. He still had a glimpse of hope. He didn't know why, but he did. Patrick made it through basic training and there wasn't a day, he didn't think of Miriam. He wrote her every day, but never mailed the letters. He kept them in a shoe box and vowed that one day she would read them, as his wife.

Basic training was over and Patrick got two weeks of leave before he had to report to his new duty station. He was going to see his mother, but he decided to go to Philadelphia, first. He had to know. He had to see if she was happy. Patrick stepped off the bus and again walked to Woolworth's. He was praying and hoping, but knew it probably wasn't possible for Miriam to be back at work there.

She should be married now and he was sure her husband didn't allow her to work.

Patrick walked in and sat at his usual seat. No Miriam. He was disappointed, but decided what the hell, he might as well order something for the road. Patrick was digging in his bag and couldn't believe his ears.

"Would you like the meatloaf special?"

He looked up and saw Miriam. His heart skipped a beat.

"Patrick, what are you doing here?"

"What are you doing here?" he replied. "I just finished basic training and have furlough for two weeks. I had to come and see if you really did it. I thought you had quit."

"I did," she replied. "It's a long story," she said.

"I have nothing but time, and no one else is here." He smiled. The counter was empty, except for Patrick.

Miriam looked away and began speaking slowly. "After you left, I didn't know what to do. My father refused to let me see or talk to you. I was so hurt. He made me quit working, also. He said some really mean things."

She grunted and continued, "Anyway, the night before I was to be married, my fiancé went out with a couple of his friends to celebrate. I was waiting at the church the next morning, and he never showed up. I couldn't believe it. Here, I was confused, but still going to marry him, even though I had feelings for someone else, as well; and then he had the nerve not to show up." She cried softly.

Patrick's heart was hurting for her. He would kill him for hurting her. He remained calm though, as she continued talking.

"Everyone starting whispering and looking around wondering what was going on when the wedding was running late. Finally, my parents came to me and told me to sit down that they had some news. My fiancé had been killed the night before at some bar. He was drunk and got into it with some men over something and they killed him. I never found out what that something was, but knowing my fiancé, he was running off at the mouth and was probably gambling and then didn't want to pay up. He was a sweet man until he drank and gambled. It led to his death. I was devastated. I had to get out of the house. I begged my dad, to let me go back to work and he finally agreed. I pleaded for my job back and end of story."

"Oh, no, Miriam, I'm sorry to hear about your fiancé, but I would've killed him myself, if he'd left you at the altar. I'm sorry to speak ill of the dead, but it's true."

Patrick smiled.

Miriam wiped her face and shook her head. "You haven't changed one bit."

Patrick smiled thinking of the old memory.

Miracle didn't understand. He went through hell to get this woman and he would be damned, if he would let his memory forget her. The thought killed him a little inside each day. He would fight this thing, whatever it was, to the end. He refused to let the sweet, sweet memory of his Miriam die.

He was a Marine. Semper Fi—Fight to the end or die trying.

Chapter Eighteen

Miracle

Miracle was glad to be home. *Even though her life was crazy and hectic—each and every day, she missed it, while she was away.* She couldn't believe she had just let the thought cross her mind, but it was true.

As much as I complain about all that I do, it makes me who I am, she thought.

I have become a stronger person, negotiator, and Lord knows I have more patience. Don't get it twisted. At times, I want to run like hell, away from everyone and everything.

That's why it's great to get away at times, she laughed.

But she couldn't imagine what her life would be like without her family and all of the craziness.

She took a deep breath before she entered her refuge and madhouse—all in one. She knew the kids would have a million and one questions and requests before she could even set her bags down. Mychal would be expecting some good loving before the night was over and who knows, what Dad needed. She plastered on her happy face and walked in the door to prepare herself for the raft of what was to come from being gone a few days.

As expected, as soon as she walked in, it began right away. Of course, after the greetings and pleasantries, Mason and McKenzie started filling her in on what they needed and all of the upcoming events they had to attend. Miracle just smiled and took it all in. *No rest for the weary.*

"Okay, guys," Mychal interjected. "You're making it seem like I didn't handle anything, while mom was away."

Mason and McKenzie both looked at each other, giggled, then back to their mother.

"Mom," they both said.

Miracle just smiled. "I got it," she responded. "Just give me a minute to get my things upstairs and we can discuss it a little later. You guys didn't even ask about your Uncle Joey."

She shook her head.

"Sorry, mom," they both said in unison.

Even though they were a few years apart in age they were so much alike, that they spoke at the same time and completed each other's sentences, at times. It was funny because they fought all the time, too, but they had a bond no one could break.

"How is Uncle Joey?" McKenzie managed to get out first.

"He's coming around," Miracle said. "It's a really tough time for him. He will make it through with time. You guys should call him some time. I'm sure hearing from you would brighten his day."

"I don't know what to say," Mason said. "I can't imagine losing your spouse."

"Yeah, mom, I wouldn't know what to say," McKenzie added.

"Just be yourself," Miracle smiled. "All he needs is love and support from his family. He loves you guys, so anything you say will help him. Just be sincere and speak from your heart."

Miracle got up to take her things upstairs. She didn't want to focus on this conversation too long, because she didn't want them to start asking too many questions or mentioning things that didn't need to be said before she had talked to Mychal. The kids knew their uncle got married six months ago, but it wasn't revealed to them either that Tracey was a he.

She had a pretty good idea that Mason knew, but she didn't want to deal with it right now. Mason had asked her years ago, if Uncle Joey was gay. She didn't deny or confirm it. Miracle shunned him off, not wanting to answer an uncomfortable question. Mason left it alone, but he knew. He dared not say anything, but he knew. He could tell when his mom avoided questions, she didn't want to answer.

It didn't matter to him anyway. He loved his uncle and nothing else mattered. He figured his dad didn't know, because his mom quickly changed the subject every time the possibility came up that Uncle Joey was gay. Mason learned to keep his mouth shut on the topic. He knew better. His mother was mild mannered, but she had another side, as well and he didn't want to see it unnecessarily. He learned it the hard way.

Miracle stood up again and walked over to her luggage. Mychal grabbed her luggage and headed upstairs.

"So, what's been going on?" Miracle asked.

"Same old, same old," he said.

"Did you talk to Aaron?"

"Yeah, I talked to that…"

Miracle shot him a look before he could get it out.

"Mychal, please, not now. I don't feel like hearing you go off about Aaron. I just got back. I need a hot shower and a few minutes to get myself together."

"I wasn't going to say anything bad," he lied.

"Yeah, right," she replied. "I just want to know if you got the time off, so we can attend the funeral."

"Yes, Miracle, I got the time off," he sighed. "It couldn't be at a worse time, but I got it off."

"Well, excuse the heck out of me," she retorted. "I told God to take Tracey home now, just to inconvenience you."

She didn't want to do this now. *Please, don't let this man get on my nerves this fast,* she was thinking.

I haven't even been in the house thirty minutes, yet. She took a deep breath and starting preparing for her shower.

Mychal walked over to Miracle and took her in close. He

looked her in the face and kissed her.

"I don't want to argue," he said.

Mychal had needs and didn't want this to turn into a night leading to no sex for him, so he figured he would smooth this over, now. It had been days since he released his manhood and he sure the hell wasn't going to let that damn Aaron keep him from getting the goodies.

Hell, naw! He'd been looking forward to tonight, all day.

"Go take your shower. I will handle everything else for the evening," he said. "I don't want you stressed tonight. I need you relaxed and focused for this loving I'm going put on you," he joked.

"Oh, really!" she smiled.

"Yes, Ma'am!" he replied. "Girl, I've been saving up for this all day. You're going to be in trouble. So, take your pretty butt and get in the shower and let the hot water rinse away all your worries and then, Big Daddy will be back to handle the rest."

"We'll see about that," Miracle replied smugly.

"Oh, yes, we will."

He hit Miracle on the butt and walked out of the bedroom.

Miracle smiled, but knew Mychal had a hidden agenda. He wanted sex—plain and simple. She knew her husband, all too well. He needs his loving like clockwork.

He will go to any cost to avoid an argument, if it means no sex for the night. They could be in a heated debate, but he would clean it up quick, if it meant no sex.

Ridiculous, she thought.

It boggled her mind how his little head, could think for his whole body. It was amazing how powerful it was. If all women really knew the power they had over men, this world would probably be different.

She had to laugh.

Although, Miracle had to admit it, she needed some loving herself. No matter what she was going through, once the love making began, her world seemed beatable. She could face and conquer it once her husband made her feel wanted and sexy. He knew exactly what to do to make her feel powerful. They had a connection so deep—sexually—that it was scary. He knew all the right buttons to push to elevate her body into empyreal. She shuddered, just thinking of her husband's touch. She couldn't be mad at his "oh, so, obvious reason for not wanting to argue." Hell, she needed it too. His love making always rejuvenated and revitalized her.

Miracle had some tough issues on the rise, so any opportunity to suppress it, just for a little while, was worth it, to her. Besides, she knew Mychal wasn't going to be happy, once he found out that she had been withholding information. Okay, lying to him.

She figured she'd sex him up real good, and maybe, just maybe, it would take away some of the sting of her not telling him about Tracey. She tried to convince herself, even though she knew it wasn't true.

Miracle walked into the bathroom, turned on the shower and disrobed. She stepped in the shower and let the hot water run down her body and rinse her troubles down the drain—for now.

However, what she didn't know was that Mychal had a secret, too. They both had been keeping secrets.

Would they both be willing to forgive one another? Only time would tell.

Chapter Nineteen

Miracle

Miracle couldn't believe how quickly the week had gone by. She had been working night and day trying to catch up with all the work she missed while away and it was time for her to leave again to attend the funeral. Thank goodness, she had the flexibility to work anywhere. Her finance degree helped her land her dream job with a commercial investment company who purchased properties and converted them into condos and apartments in up and coming areas. Miracle was almost close to receiving her commercial real estate license, as well. She decided to get her license, so she could know everything about the business from both angles—the finance and the property side. She was sitting at the computer in the office crunching numbers when the phone rang.

"Hello," Miracle answered.

"Hey, Miracle, did I catch you at a bad time?" Karma asked.

"No, Karma. Just working, but I could use a break."

Miracle felt bad, because she wanted to call Karma when she got home, but the week had slipped by her and she was so busy. She had good intentions, but figured she would get through the funeral and then focus on Karma.

"How are you doing?" Miracle asked. "Sorry, I didn't call you when I got back, but things have been crazy."

"Girl, you don't have to explain. Trust me, I understand. Husband, work and children are enough to make anyone crazy and you try to be superwoman," Karma laughed.

"You can say that again," Miracle sighed. "Honey, I need to have an "S" on my chest."

They both laughed.

"But right now, it's not about me. How are you doing?" Miracle asked.

"I'm hanging. It's a thin strand some days, but I'm still hanging. That's all I can do," she added. "You won't believe what this fool did," Karma said. "He had the nerve to show up here, while I'm lying in this hospital bed with cancer that I got from his smoking, to ask me to sign divorce papers, so he can move on with his life."

Miracle gasped. "Karma, you are lying. I know that man... Lord, Jesus I almost said something else, didn't bring his butt up there and do that. What! He has a lot of damn nerve. Are you kidding me? He needs to burn in hell for this one."

"Right," said Karma. "But I actually feel a little sorry for him." She added, "For anyone to be so selfish, they have to be miserable. He has some serious issues that he needs to face and I don't care how long he continues to run, his life will never be right, until he faces those demons. Believe it or not I still pray for him. I know it sounds crazy, but I do." She admitted.

"Well, I must confess, I think you are a better woman than me. I'm not sure if I would be able to pray for him. It would be very difficult. I don't wish harm on anyone, but girl, if it was me, God would have to work real hard on me. I'm just being honest."

"You say that, Miracle, but I know you," Karma speculated. "I don't see you wishing ill will on anyone."

"Huh! If you say so," Miracle laughed. "I do have a devilish side, Trust and believe it," she confirmed.

"In that case, I'm going to pray for you too." Karma

laughed and seemed to be in good spirits, today.

"Shoot, I hope you are already praying for me. Girl, you have a direct connect and a sista can sure use that type of prayer. What did you do when he handed you the divorce papers?" Miracle asked.

"After the shock wore off, I told him to leave. I couldn't believe he had the balls to do it. I kindly told him to get out. He tried to give me some tired explanation, but I wasn't trying to hear it."

"Are you going to sign them?" Miracle asked.

"I…"

Before Karma could answer, Patrick walked into the office.

"Miracle, we need to talk," Patrick interjected.

"Karma, can I call you back, a bit later."

"Oh, I'm sorry. I didn't realize you were on the phone," Patrick whispered.

Miracle held up her finger signaling for him to wait.

"Okay, girl, I'll call you back, a bit later. Talk to you, soon." Miracle hung up the phone.

"What's up, dad?"

"Baby girl, I'm not going to be able to go tomorrow. I just can't bring myself to face Joseph. We haven't spoken in years. I don't think I should show up."

"Dad, I disagree. I think this is the best time to show up. Joseph is your son and he is hurting. He lost the love of his life. For you to swallow your pride and show up, would mean the world to him, I'm sure."

"Huh, I don't know about that," Patrick snidely said. "The last time I saw Joseph, he told me that he never had to see me ever again. Don't you remember what he said?" he asked. "Joseph said some pretty terrible things to me."

"If I recall, you both said some pretty ugly things." Miracle added. "Both of you are stubborn and bullheaded. Someone has to give. One of you has to be the bigger person and make this relationship right. You only have one son and you're not getting any younger, dad, you should want to make this right, before it's too late. I'm sure this is what mom would have wanted. It would have broken her heart to see you and Joey not speaking. The whole thing is foolish. There should be nothing that serious keeping you from being in your son's life. But you don't want to budge or give in. It's just crazy to me. I do know this much, Joey is truly hurting and he could use all the support he can get during this time."

Patrick turned his head and looked out the window. "He probably doesn't even want me there, anyway," he protested.

"Well, you won't know unless you're willing to go. Dad, you always raised us to make things right, so, how can you not even follow your own teachings. This is your son, your flesh and blood. Life's too short. This funeral is a prime example of the fact. I'm sure Joseph and Tracey didn't think six months ago that this would be the outcome for them. I purchased your ticket any way with the intentions of you going. It's up to you. You know where I stand and how I feel. However, I can't force you to attend. You are my father, even though right now you're not acting like it." She smiled.

Patrick knew she was right, but he didn't want to admit it. Joseph had really hurt him with the words he spoke when they had that last encounter. Patrick knew he had said some harsh words, as well, but they were true. At least, they were his truths.

Joseph had some nerve. Patrick could still remember the blow up…

Miriam had just passed away and they were preparing for her funereal. Joseph wanted to attend the funeral with his lover and Patrick wouldn't hear of it.

"You will not disrespect your mother or the church by bringing a man as your significant other," Patrick shouted.

"Why not, dad? Get over it, your son is gay, dad. Yes, dad, I'm gay. I know you have been denying it for years, but it's not going away. Mom accepted me. Why can't you?" Joseph fumed. "I know she wouldn't have a problem with me attending with Tracey. She loved Tracey."

"That's your mother!" Patrick retorted.

"Yes, you're right, she is my mother. The one who loves me, no matter what or whom I love? I'm sure, if it was the other way around and you were the one dead, mom wouldn't have a problem with me bringing him to your funeral."

Patrick was heated now. He couldn't believe his own son would say something so hurtful to him. This was the child he raised and protected from the world. Is this what he really thought? After all the times he saved his ass from all of the reckless behavior he displayed as a teenager and a young adult. He couldn't count the number of times he bailed this boy out of trouble—literally and figuratively.

Joseph regretted what he had said, the moment it left his lips, but it was already out in the atmosphere. He truly loved his father and wanted his support more than anything in the world. It shook him to the core that he didn't have his support. The one person, who he wanted to be accepted by, was the one that despised his lifestyle the most. He was heartbroken, so he wanted his father to feel the same pain.

It hurt him terribly though, because he never disrespected his parents. He had done a lot of things, but disrespect was not one of them. However, his passion for his lifestyle was so strong that this one time, he was willing to make an exception, if it would influence his father's decision to see things his way.

But... It didn't work. Instead this display of contempt only made matters worse. He felt awful, but he was too stubborn to apologize. He wanted the sting of his words to hurt his dad, the same way he was hurting.

"You don't have to come at all," Patrick shouted. "We can bury your mother without you and your fairy." Patrick shot back with fury.

Patrick was hot as fish grease and knew he was about to lose it. How dare he fix his mouth to wish death on his own father? "As far as I'm concerned, since I should be dead, you're dead to me." Patrick regretted his words, as well, once they left his lips, but it was way too late. He'd let Joseph rally up that ugly monster in his soul and it wasn't pretty.

Once the words are spoken, it's hard to take them back—Patrick and Joseph, both, knew it.

The conversation was over at that point. Neither said

another word.

Joseph attended the funeral alone and left immediately after the services. He didn't utter one word to his father, the entire time he was there.

Miracle was devastated. Not only did she lose her mother, but now her father and brother weren't speaking. It was too much to handle.

This was the time that she needed them both and they wanted to kill each other.

Patrick didn't try to speak with Joseph, either. This was the last time they spoke or saw one another... three years ago.

After a few minutes, which seemed like a lifetime, Patrick turned back to Miracle. Deep down he wanted to go, because he knew he should make things right with Joseph, but he didn't know how. Enough time had gone by and he missed his son. He loved Joseph—he just didn't love all the choices he made for his life. Patrick was realizing now, that it's okay to love someone and still not agree with some of the things they chose to do in their lives.

"Let me sleep on it," he told Miracle. "I will let you know my decision in the morning."

"Okay, dad," she smiled.

She was going to leave it alone. Miracle knew that it ate at him—little by little. She really did want to fix it, but this was something the two of them would have to work out for themselves. She could help lead them in the right direction, but it's ultimately up to them to make this right.

"I'll let you get back to work," Patrick said.

"Dad, is there something else you want to tell me?"

"Uhm... what?" Patrick asked.

"Did anything happen, while I was away that I need to know about?"

"Nope. Don't have a clue what you're talking about."

"Okay, dad. You know what I'm talking about. The police were here and things were a little crazy. Mychal already filled me in on the story. I'll let it slide for now, because we have enough to deal with for tomorrow, but trust me, we will be discussing it. I'm going to schedule an appointment with your doctor, when we return. Dad, please take the time to seriously consider both of these circumstances and make a rational decision that will be good for all involved. I love you, dad."

"I love you, too, baby."

Patrick turned and walked out of the office.

Miracle smiled. She knew that he would make the right choice. When it came to his family in the long run, he always did.

Chapter Twenty

Miracle

Miracle didn't sleep well, at all last night. She dreamed of Joey, the funeral and the secrets that she kept from Mychal. She knew she should at least fess up about Joey and his spouse before they made it to Atlanta, but for some reason she could not fix her mouth and brain to cooperate. It was the morning of the funeral and they would be in ATL real soon. She was scared.

Miracle got up to go to the bathroom. The mirror stopped Miracle in her tracks. She looked at her brown face and felt ashamed.

What happened? Who was she?

She knew this was a dangerous game she was playing. Keeping secrets always leads to trouble. She washed her face to try and wash away some of the guilt.

It didn't work.

Mychal was still sleeping peacefully. Miracle cuddled up to Mychal. She shook him gently to wake him up. Mychal turned over to face Miracle.

"Good morning," he smiled.

"Morning," she volunteered. "We need to talk."

He sat up in the bed to face Miracle. He ran his hands over his face to wake up. He looked puzzled.

"I don't even know where to begin," she confessed.

"What's up, Miracle? Just say it," he said.

She wanted to tell him everything; both Karma and Joey's situation.

Which one is less damaging? She wondered, *which should I expose first?*

She didn't want to get him too upset and then he would refuse to attend the funeral with her today. She really needed her husband to be there.

I need his strength to make it through.

Miracle knew Joey was going to be a mess today. Mychal's strength was going to be what she needed to be strong for Joseph. Without it, they both would be a hot mess.

"When was the last time you spoke with Karma?" she asked.

"Funny you should ask, because I was thinking of her the other day. I meant to call her."

A flash of Walter and the woman sitting at the restaurant revisited his mind.

"Actually, I was going to go see her because I saw Walter last week, when I went to pick up the food for the kids. I had been meaning to tell you, but things have been so hectic this last week, I didn't have a chance."

"Walter was there? Really!"

"Yeah, and you won't believe this shit," he said. "He was sitting in the back corner at a table with some damn woman, who wasn't my sister."

Mychal grabbed his phone from the nightstand and pulled up the pictures he had snapped.

Miracle tried to look shocked.

"Maybe, it was just a friend," Miracle added.

"I don't think so, babe. No man hides in a corner of a place with a woman who is just a friend when he's married. Besides, they were holding and rubbing hands. Oh, trust and believe she wasn't a damn friend. I started to go over there and whip his ass. Somehow, I held it together. It took everything in my power, but I just chilled. When we get back, I'm going to go see Karma. I wanted to call her, but I know I wouldn't be able to hold it inside. This is something that should be handled face-to-face. Hopefully, she won't get mad, for me not telling her sooner, but I need to tell her. I can't have my sister around here looking like a fool, while her husband is sleeping around. Not on my watch."

"What if she already knows?" Miracle asked turning away.

"Huh! Why would you say that?"

"Just a question," she replied.

She wouldn't look at Mychal.

"No, there is a reason you asked the question. I know you, Miracle."

"It was just a question," she said. Her voice became pitchy. "I'm just thinking out loud that's all."

"Your mind doesn't operate like that and besides, who asks a question like that out of the blue. When was the last time you spoke to Karma?" he asked.

Miracle still wasn't looking at Mychal. "No, Mir," he said. "Look at me."

Miracle finally turned and faced him. Tears began to roll down her cheeks. Mychal got out of the bed and paced the floor.

"Miracle, don't tell me you know about this," he asked.

"Well, I... I," she stammered.

"So, Karma already knows this clown is cheating on her? I knew I should have whipped his ass in the restaurant."

Mychal was getting upset all over again. This time he was angry with himself. He should have followed his gut feeling.

"Miracle, how could you not tell me? No secrets, right? I thought we had no secrets."

"Mychal, you have to understand. Let me explain." She got out of the bed and walked over to him. "Will you calm down? First of all, and please, stop pacing the floor, you're going to walk a hole in the carpet," she smiled.

She was trying to calm him down, before she revealed more.

"Karma told me, but she asked me not to say anything. I know you may feel it's wrong; however, I was just doing what

I was asked. She came to me in confidence and asked me not to tell anyone."

"I'm not anyone!" he shot back. "I'm your husband."

"Yes, you are my husband, but you are also her brother. We both know how you can get, so we thought it was best, at the time, not to tell you. Trust me, it has been bothering me and I had just told Karma that I was going to tell you everything, when I got back from Atlanta. I hated keeping it from you, but I gave her my word and that means a lot to me. There were plenty of times I wanted to tell you but I couldn't."

"Okay, back up. What do you mean everything? Is there more, Miracle? Please, don't tell me he put his hands on my sister. I will definitely kill him."

Mychal hit the dresser with his fist. Miracle jumped.

"Mychal, please!" she retorted.

"No, he has not put his hands on her. I would never keep that a secret. I would have beat his ass myself, if that was the case."

Mychal raised his eyebrow. "Well, what else is it?"

Miracle took a deep breath. She didn't know how to say it. The affair was bad enough, but she didn't know how he would take the cancer thing. She really wished Karma would have been the one to tell him this news.

"Karma is sick." She managed to say.

"Sick. What do you mean sick?"

"She has cancer."

"Cancer. How? When?"

Mychal sat down in the chair at the end of the bed and grabbed his head in his hands. He held back his tears. He felt terrible.

His sister has cancer and is dealing with a cheating husband and he didn't have a clue. It was like a blow to his stomach. It upset him that he had been so busy he hadn't taken the time to check on her, to make sure all was well. Life has a way of separating us from what's important. However, that's no excuse.

"Damn, this is crazy!" He sighed shaking his head. "When it rains, it pours. Here I'm just thinking she will find out Walter is a cheating-ass liar, but she's dealing with that and cancer. Why? Not Karma. She doesn't deserve this, Mir. Damn."

Miracle walked over and sat on the floor in front of him.

"Mychal, I'm sorry. I know this sucks, but unfortunately we have to play the hand we are dealt."

"I'm hurt, you didn't tell me," he confessed. "Why did you keep this from me?" he asked.

"Believe me, babe, I wanted to tell you, but Karma said she needed time. It happened so quickly. One day she was fine and then the next, she finds out she has cancer and on top of it all, Walter's cheating—after they've been married for twenty years. You must admit, it is a big pill to swallow, all at once. She didn't know what to do. Her world was shattered. It wasn't like we were keeping it from you on purpose. She just needed some time and space to dissect the information and figure out what she was going to do. She was devastated. Her world was turned upside down. I just happened to be the person she confided in, to help her make some sense of it all—to be a listening ear without judgment."

"Oh, so, now I can't be a listening ear?" he asked.

Miracle gave him a look. "Really, Mychal? You would have been over there trying to stump Walter into the ground. Secondly, you would worry Karma to no end. She just wanted some time to let it sink in, analyze the situation and then figure out how to proceed. We all react differently to situations; however, we must recognize and respect other's decisions. That's all I was doing. I wanted to tell you, but I couldn't, at least, not at the time. Trust me, it wasn't what I wanted and I hated keeping it from you. Please, say you understand? I'm sure there has been a time when you wanted to tell me something, but it just wasn't the right time, or vowed you would never mention it again, unless absolutely necessary. Is it right? No, but we all do it, at times."

Mychal stiffened a little. She had hit a nerve. He knew the feeling all too well. Maybe, he needed to let this go. It wasn't about him, anyway. It was about Karma. His wife was who she was and people confided in her, because they knew that her word was her bond. If she said that she wasn't going to tell anyone's story, then she wasn't. She stood firm on her gift as a listener and confidant.

Folks in glass houses can't throw stones, he thought.

There was something that he was compressing deep down inside of himself. Even though it happened many years ago, before they were married, it haunted him from time-to-time.

"It took a lot for me to tell you. I told Karma that I was going to tell you. Of course, it would have been better, if she had told you, but I didn't like keeping this secret. We spoke while I was in Atlanta and I informed her that I was going to tell you. It was hard for me, but I explained to her it made me uncomfortable that I knew and you didn't. It was okay at first, but it was getting hard for me to see her going through this and not have your support. She needs all the support she can get, right now."

"I bet she does, since her sorry ass, no good husband walked out on her and the kids. The kids. How are they? Where are they?"

"They are fine. Karma's neighbor has been helping out."

"I've got to get over there when we get back from Atlanta. I'm going to call her; no, I want to see her. Hell, I don't know what to do."

He stood up and started pacing again. Miracle got up and stopped her husband. She grabbed him and hugged him tightly. He was hurting and didn't know what to do.

"Mychal, it's okay, baby. We will get through this, as we always do. Karma is a strong woman. Her faith in God is unwavering. She is leaning on Him and trusting in Him to see her through. Let's focus on Joseph and this funeral. When we get back we can then turn our full attention to Karma. One day and one hurdle, at a time," she observed.

She grabbed his face and kissed his lips.

He smiled a little. "I hear you, babe. Thank you," he mumbled.

"Babe, it's one thing after another. It's Life," she responded.

"One more thing," he said. "We can't forget about the elephant in the house," he said.

Miracle looked confused. "What's that?" she said.

"Your dad," he replied.

Was it ever going to end, she thought!

Chapter Twenty-One

Miracle

Miracle and Mychal were ready to go and had their luggage at the door. They were waiting for the car to arrive to take them to the airport.

She didn't know if Patrick was going. He hadn't said anything more about it, since they had talked.

Her phone rang and it was the car service saying the driver would be there in less than ten minutes.

"The car will be here in a few minutes," she told Mychal.

"Cool," he said. "I forgot something, be right back," he said. He ran upstairs.

Miracle was playing everything through her head, making sure she didn't forget anything. Rosita was picking up the kids. She believed she had everything. As she was thinking, Patrick came walking towards her with his luggage.

"Good morning," she said.

"Good morning," he responded.

"Glad to see you." She smiled.

"Yeah," Patrick replied.

He didn't have much to say. This was very difficult for him. This was a big step for him and Miracle knew it.

"Good morning, dad," Mychal said, as he came down the stairs. He looked at Miracle.

She just smiled.

They arrived in Atlanta with just enough time to check into the hotel, freshen up and get ready for the funeral.

"You know, I hate funerals," Mychal confessed.

"Well, babe, I don't think anyone really enjoys them," she replied.

"I don't know about that," he laughed. You remember my Aunt Judith, she loves them. She would go to people's funerals that she didn't even know."

"Stop it!" Miracle laughed.

"No, I'm serious," he said. "The woman would be sitting up in funerals of folks she didn't know from Adam. Crying and everything," he added.

"Mychal, please!" She giggled. "Now, that's crazy. What in the world? Who would want to attend a funeral of someone they didn't know? It's hard enough to make it through funerals of people you do know."

"Baby, I don't know, but I'm telling you the truth. Folks started calling her, 'Judith the Undertaker.' Don't make me call my mom," he joked.

"Boy, I have to finish getting dressed and you are holding me up," Miracle chuckled.

Mychal was trying to lighten the mood. He knew this was going to be a traumatic day for his wife. He wanted to give her a few laughs, before it became too serious.

Miracle shook her head and finished getting ready. She knew Mychal was just trying to give her a few laughs before all hell broke loose. It worked for now.

Patrick, Mychal and Miracle arrived at the funeral. There were people piling in already. The limo was pulling up in front of the building. The windows were tinted so dark, they couldn't see inside. Miracle assumed, it was Joseph and Tracey's parents. She was right. Joseph rolled down the window.

"Miracle," he called.

She walked over to the limo. Mark was sitting next to Joseph and Tracey's parents were sitting opposite them.

"Hello," she said as she stuck her head in the window to kiss Joey on his cheek. He had on sunglasses to cover his blood shot eyes, she imagined.

"Wait at the door," he said. "I want you guys to walk in with us," he said.

Joseph hadn't seen his father, yet.

Miracle said a quick prayer that things wouldn't get ugly at this funeral. It wasn't the time or the place for it.

"Okay," she responded. "Uhm… Joseph, I need to tell you something," she said.

"Let me get out first," he replied. He was already opening the door. Miracle wanted to tell him before he exited the limo, but it was too late. Joseph was stepping out before she could say another word.

"Please, Lord," she murmured under her breath. Patrick and Mychal were standing a few feet away.

Joseph got out and asked, "Where is Mychal? I thought you said he was coming with you."

He was looking around. Joseph's heart dropped. He saw Mychal and his father.

He quickly looked back at Miracle. "Mir… no you didn't," he said in a low controlled voice. "What the hell is he doing here?"

"Joey, please! Not, now. He's here because he loves you and wants to support you."

"Huh," Joey responded. "I doubt that. It's been a long time. People who love you don't go years without trying to repair the relationship."

"You're right, Joey, but it goes both ways."

"I wasn't the one who said that I didn't love him." He shot back.

"Joey, not now, let's not do this here," she said through

smiled lips. People started noticing the exchange between them.

Mychal walked over. "Is everything okay?"

"Yes, babe, it's fine. Joseph wants us to walk in with him."

"I want the two of you to walk in with me, not him," he said pointing to Patrick.

"Joseph, come on man, we don't want to cause a scene right here. The funeral hasn't even started, yet." Mychal tried to reason.

"Oh, it's not going to be a scene and he's not walking in with me."

Patrick could see something was going on, but couldn't hear the exchange. He figured it was about him, since Joseph kept staring in his direction and pointing his fingers. Patrick just walked into the church.

I will find a seat in the back, he said to himself. *Hell, I don't want to be here no more than you want me here,* he thought.

He was lying to himself, but if that was what it took to make him feel better, then so be it.

"Dad went inside," Miracle responded.

"No, your dad went inside," he said. "He stopped being my dad a long time ago."

The funeral director walked over and informed Joseph that it was time to go inside.

Miracle was so caught up in dealing with Joey acting like a twelve-year old that she totally forgot she was going to inform Mychal that Tracey was a "he."

After the whole Karma ordeal, she couldn't get into the Joey thing, right then. What was the big deal anyway? Mychal would just have to get his homophobic fears in check to make it through this funeral.

Hell, I'm tired of being Saint Elizabeth.

He was a big boy and he would just have to deal with this one. She had her hands full with Joseph and making sure he wouldn't cause a scene with their father.

They walked in and passed Patrick, who was sitting in a seat in the rear of the church. The place was packed. There were flowers everywhere. It was a floral explosion. They were beautiful.

Joseph was in front, Mark and Miracle walked side by side, Tracey parents were next and Mychal bought up the rear. Joseph made it to the front and Tracey was lying there looking like a prince. He had a slight smile on his face. Joseph vowed that he would keep it together. He bent down and kissed Tracey on the lips. He took his seat in the front row. Mark and Miracle sat next to him. Tracey's parents viewed their son for the last time. Tracey's mom kissed her baby boy. Her second child had left this earth, before her. She started crying softly. Her husband led her to their seats, as she sobbed.

Mychal made it to the mahogany silk lined coffin and looked down. He stumbled when he saw the stiff body lying there.

Were his eyes playing tricks on him? It couldn't be? What the fuck? He thought.

No way. He lingered at the coffin for a bit too long. Miracle got up and walked next to him.

"You okay?" she asked.

Mychal didn't even notice or hear Miracle. She gently shook his arm.

Oh no! She thought.

Mychal turned and faced Miracle. "Huh," he said.

"Please, come sit down."

Miracle said a quick prayer to keep Mychal in check. All she needed was for him to cause a scene, now. She knew he was pissed because Tracey was a he and not a she.

He walked over to the pew with Miracle and sat down. He stared blankly at the casket the whole time, while the funeral director and his assistants prepared to seal the casket. The ushers began handing out the obituary. One of the ushers was trying to hand Mychal a program, but he was still staring at the casket and didn't even notice her.

Miracle took his program. She knew that he was pissed, but something seemed odd. Mychal was looking like he saw a ghost. She knew he would be shocked by Tracey being a man and upset because he was white. But there was something else going on. Miracle could sense it.

She gave him his program. He knew the program would confirm his suspension. He opened it up slowly and began reading the bio. Mychal closed the program and caught one last glimpse of Tracey, as the funeral director sealed the casket and cranked it closed.

Mychal didn't hear anything during the entire service. Mychal was elusive for the remainder of the trip.

Chapter Twenty-Two

Mychal

Immediately... his mind flashed him back to that night many years ago. He was a junior in college and on top of his game on the court. He was the man. All of the women wanted him and he could have anyone he wanted.

Mychal wanted Miracle. They had met freshman year and he had been after her ever since. They had become good friends, but she never let it go any further. He pursued her—relentlessly. She had finally agreed to give him a chance, after three years; and he was excited.

He had his share of women, but Miracle was different. She was wifey material. All of those other girls were just booty calls and ratchets. He knew they only wanted to be with him because he was a guarantee for the NBA. His parents had warned him about fake women. He wasn't turning down the booty, though. He was young and sex is sex. However, Miracle was always on his mind and heart. She had him, even if he didn't want to admit it. She agreed to go out with him and he knew that one date was all he needed and he would have her.

Miracle got to his dorm room for their date a little early, because she had finished earlier than expected with her group. The library was near his dorm, so she just figured she would head over there, instead of going back to her dorm. They were not in the same dorm any more. He was in the dorm for the athletes. She knocked on the door and his roommate let her in.

"Is Mychal here?"

"Yeah, he's in his room," his roommate said. His roommate was at the table trying to study and wasn't really paying attention to anything else. He was cussing and trying to understand some math book he was looking at. She laughed and shook her head.

Jocks, she thought.

Miracle knocked on Mychal's door and opened it up like many times before. However, what she saw made her sick. Mychal was standing there and a girl was on her knees with all that the good Lord gave him in her mouth. He had his eyes closed, but when Miracle gasped, he opened them and almost fell. The bad part was that the chick on her knees didn't even stop. Mychal pushed her off of him and she fell back.

Miracle ran out of the dorm. He wanted to chase after her, but he couldn't really do that right now with his penis hanging out.

Damn it, he thought.

He threw the girl out of his room and was so pissed he didn't know what to do.

He had messed up—bad. She would never be with him. His second head always got him in trouble.

The next day, after Mychal's game he tried to talk to Miracle at a party. She wanted nothing to do with him. Mychal started drinking and drank more than normal. He wasn't a big drinker; he was always worried about being in tip-top shape for his sport. He didn't like the way alcohol made him feel. He felt it always clouded his judgment.

Tonight, he didn't care. He didn't want to feel anything. Miracle was gone. He had screwed up. Some of the players from the opposing team that they had played earlier were at the party. Mychal started talking to this guy, who was a good player and had given him a run for his money on the court. His game was pretty tight for a white boy. Mychal had to respect his game.

The other player was a fan and had been following Mychal's basketball journey, since high school. Mychal was well-known and people were drawn to him. It was a relief for Mychal to talk about basketball, instead of worrying about losing Miracle. His new friend was a fan. Mychal relaxed as they reviewed some of his best games and shared stories about behind the scene tricks, which made the difference between winning and losing. They had a lot in common.

At this point, Mychal was two shades to the wind. The music was pumping and so was Mychal's head. He had started confiding in this stranger.

The stranger was totally attentive and was a great listener, he thought.

"I need to get out of here," Mychal mumbled. The smell of alcohol and the beat of the music had his head swirling. He was going to vomit. There was no way in hell Mychal Alexander would dare show weakness in front of a crowd—he was the big man on campus. He almost hit the floor as he stood. The stranger grabbed Mychal and led him to the door. His grip was hard and comforting at the same time. The alcohol had him tripping. He felt a tinge of excitement when the stranger had pulled him close. The other player was excited to be alone with Mychal Alexander that he would do anything.

They left the party. Mychal was not in the best of shape. He tried to act like he was good, but he really wasn't. He legs were wobbly and his words were slurred. The stranger had to help him walk.

"Where do you want to go?" the stranger asked.

"My dorm," Mychal urged.

"I can't believe this," Mychal whispered.

"What's wrong?" the stranger inquired.

"I screwed up. I lost my wife. No, he lost my wife," he said angrily pointing to his crotch.

Mychal knew he was talking way too much, but he couldn't

stop. The alcohol had his lips loose.

They reached Mychal's dorm. The stranger released Mychal and turned to leave.

"Take care, man. I hope things work out for you," the stranger comforted.

"Come in," Mychal demanded.

The dorm room was dark, except for a desk lamp on in the corner. His roommate was probably still partying and celebrating the win. The room was spacious and setup like a two-bedroom apartment. There was a main living area and both guys had rooms opposite each other with their own bathroom.

"I have to vomit," Mychal said, as he stumbled and almost fell—again.

"Where's the bathroom?" the stranger asked.

"My bathroom is over to the left in my room." The stranger helped him get to his room. Mychal ran to the bathroom and ejected most of the contents of his stomach. He suddenly felt much better. He cleaned himself up.

The player from the other team was sitting in a chair in the corner of Mychal's room. He had the bluest eyes Mychal had ever seen. It surprised him that he opened up to this dude. There was something about him, which made talking to him come with ease.

"Hey, thanks, man, for helping me out. I don't usually drink so much," Mychal admitted.

"Yeah, I kind of figured it out already," he smiled.

"Yeah, it was just a rough day and I guess I figured I could drink away the pain. However, I've learned it doesn't work. I feel like I played five games non-stop without any hydration and the hurt is still there, so it wasn't even worth it," he laughed.

"Oh, trust me, I know. I've been there a couple times myself," he replied.

"Drinking never fixes anything. It may dim the light, but after it wears off, the light is still there, if not brighter."

Something was happening and Mychal couldn't explain it. He felt really at ease with this guy. This wasn't usual for him. It must have been the alcohol. He never let strangers in his circle. He was cautious of everyone, thanks to his parents drilling it in his head.

They talked about basketball and how it excited them. Both had a mutual love for the sport. The other guy knew that he would never make it to the NBA like Mychal, but he still loved the game. It was his way to release from the stressors in his life, that's why it came so natural to relate to Mychal.

They talked more about basketball and their plans after college. Mychal didn't know what he was feeling. He was attracted to this guy for his passion about basketball and life. It was weird and he both hated it and liked it—at the same time.

The other ball player could detect that Mychal was feeling him. This was his dream. To be alone in a room with Mychal Alexander was the only thing he needed to get what he wanted. He knew Mychal wasn't gay, but he didn't care. He just wanted him—even if it was only once. He had admired this guy, since high school.

The stranger knew that his personality and skills could land Mychal, given the opportunity. The gods had been listening. When he saw Mychal at the party and watched the interaction happening between him and the women he spoke of all night, somehow, he knew this was his chance. So, he took it. He could feel that he was wearing Mychal down. He had every step calculated in his head and had to proceed exactly as planned, or he would ruin it.

"Basketball is like sex," the stranger confided. "It's fast, exciting and explosive, if played right," the stranger commented.

Mychal laughed. "You're right. I never thought of it like that. Makes sense though, since you said it. I guess that's why I love the game so much," he grinned.

The stranger walked over to Mychal and confessed, "Me, too."

He was standing inches from Mychal's face, but he didn't push him away. Instead, he felt himself getting aroused. This guy had a strange effect on him. It was like he was staring at himself, when he looked at him, but with a different skin color. They shared so much in common.

Mychal flinched when the stranger reached down and unzipped his pants, but he didn't stop him, either. Mychal's head was spinning in a million directions. The alcohol still had him woozy and his mind wasn't clear, however, he was slightly aroused.

Are you fucking kidding me? I'm not gay, he was thinking.

"Get the fuck off me!" he yelled in his mind, but no words escaped his mouth.

He was shocked that he had an erection. He had never in his life even thought about sex with another man. Yet, this felt too euphoric to stop. Mychal's breathing became shallow.

Mychal stumbled back and in his mind he was pushing the stranger away as he took all of Mychal's manhood in his mouth but physically he did nothing. Mychal cringed, but his lips felt so damn good on his penis, then, without warning, his knees went limp for a second.

The stranger's lips were the softest he had every felt in his life.

Mychal had received plenty of head, due to his stardom status; however, none felt like this, right here. He closed his eyes and imagined that it was Miracle. The thought made it bearable and the act was not so disgraceful in his mind.

What the hell was he doing? Another man had his mouth on his penis. A man!

He went back to thinking of Miracle. The orgasm Mychal experienced was so damn explosive—it made his whole body shake. He had never in his life cum so hard. It excited him more, because the stranger swallowed his soul's essences. Right now, he didn't care who it was. He just knew that he had never felt anything so damn good.

The stranger stood and began undressing. He had to have Mychal now. The anticipation was intoxicating. His body was like that of a mannequin. It was tight and right. Mychal found himself fascinated by his chiseled body.

It happened so fast that Mychal didn't see it coming. He was inside of him and the second orgasm was just as explosive, as the first. As he released his manhood, for a few seconds, all of his anxiety, worries, disappointments, successes and failures left his body. His mind was clear and he was relaxed like never before. It was both fulfilling and horrifying, at the same time.

Once Mychal collected himself, he was sickened by what had just transpired. He became serious and confused.

"I've never in my life experienced anything like that, but if you ever tell anyone what just occurred in this room, I will hunt you down like a dog and rip your heart out!"

The implications and complications of what he had just done were weighing heavy on him—like Jesus carrying the cross to his execution.

He was ashamed. He turned away from his disgust.

The other man grabbed Mychal's face and assured him that this indiscretion would never leave this room. Mychal looked in those baby blues and believed him. It was like he was peering into his own soul and his soul knew the damaging effect this secret would have on both of their lives.

"What's your name?" Mychal asked. He realized that after all this time and partaking in one of the best events in his life, so far, other than basketball, he didn't even know this dude's name.

"Tracey," he replied with a smile. He extended his hand. "Nice to meet you, Mychal," he responded.

Mychal just stared at his hand. He refused to touch him. He felt repulsed and thought he would vomit, again.

"Get the hell out," Mychal fumed.

Tracey looked hurt and confused; however, he collected his things and didn't say another word.

Mychal ran back to the bathroom and vomited—again. It was the last time he had ever laid eyes on him.

Until today!

Chapter Twenty-Three

Miracle

Mychal didn't say a word the entire flight or the ride home. Miracle knew he was upset, but she had never seen Mychal like this.

Patrick was silent, as well. He tried to reach out to Joseph, but to no avail. Joseph wanted no parts of it. Miracle told him to give Joseph some time.

"Dad, this is a tough time for him. He's dealing with a lot right now. Just give it time. The most important part is that you were there. It speaks volumes in itself," she assured him. "Joseph may not express it now, but he will one day. Trust me," she confirmed.

"I tried," he responded.

"I know and it's all we can do. Just give it time. You at least made the first step. It took a lot of courage and even if Joey doesn't appreciate it, I do." She hugged him and kissed him on his cheek.

Miracle got out of the shower and grabbed her favorite white lavender lotion and began pampering her body. The fresh scent of the lavender hit her nose and she felt mesmerized. The lavender scent always put Miracle at ease and made her feel sexy. She slipped into Mychal's favorite purple silk negligee and her body was craving her husband.

She yearned for her husband to relieve some tension. The funeral was over and now, it was time to deal with the drama at home… lying to Mychal, Karma and her dad.

She prayed the lavender scent and the skimpy negligee would get Mychal out of this funk or whatever it was. Miracle slipped into the king size bed with the 1,000 thread count silk sheets and sighed. She loved being in her own bed.

Mychal was already in bed reading a magazine. He had gone straight upstairs, when they got in the house. He had been acting strange, since the funeral.

At the repast, he didn't say much of anything. Miracle figured he would have to talk to her at some point. Well, giving him some loving always turned things around for them. Even when they were mad and not speaking to one another—sex is never withheld as punishment. They both enjoy it too much!

Miracle began rubbing her hands over Mychal's body. She could have sworn she felt his body stiffen.

Was she imaging this or did it really just happen, she thought. *No way.* She continued. Mychal grabbed her hand.

"Miracle, Stop!" he spat.

Miracle was a bit deflated. She thought for sure sex would soften the circumstances. It usually did, but they had never faced anything this serious before.

"Why didn't you tell me that Joseph was married to a man? As a matter of fact, a white man, you know how I feel about homosexuality and white people," he asked.

"I'm sorry. Trust me, Mychal, I wanted to tell you on several occasions, but the time just never seemed right. However, in the grand scheme of things now, does it really matter?"

"Hell, yes," he answered.

Miracle was a bit on the defense, now. This was her brother—her family. She loved Mychal to the core, but she was very protective of her brother.

"It just never came up. Whenever I tried to talk to you about Joey, you never seemed interested. It was like you were listening, but not hearing me when it came to him. I invited you to the wedding and I was going to tell you then, but you could care less and made all types of excuses for why you couldn't attend. My gut tells me that you knew deep down inside, but didn't want to face it; so, it was best left untouched."

Damn, he thought. She had him.

He tried to think of a response to turn the conversation back in his direction.

"Miracle, you know I had to work and that's why I couldn't go to the wedding."

"Uh huh..." she responded.

"Seriously, we had just landed a big account and everything had to be perfect," he defended.

"Mychal, it's always the same response when you want to get out of doing something you don't want to do. Work calls. That's some crap!"

"Now, my job is some crap," he retorted.

"No, sir, I didn't say that. You know what I meant," she said. "Mychal, please, I don't want to get into this now. I just want a day to decompress. All I wanted was to make love to you, which would help to relax my nerves and you're ruining my mood. What's really going on? You've been acting strange since the funeral; and it's more than the fact that Tracey was a white man. So, what's really going on?"

"Nothing is going on," he lied. "I just think it's only fair that I knew."

"Would your knowing have changed anything?" she asked.

He didn't answer.

"Exactly," she said. "You're right, I should have told you, but as I said before, I didn't really think you were interested. I was wrong and I apologize. I shouldn't have kept this from you. Mychal, I promise no more secrets."

She started touching him again. He grabbed her hand—again.

"I have one more question," he said.

"Okay," she said irritably.

"What was the cause of Tracey's death?"

His insides were churning like butter. He was trying to remain calm as Miracle spoke.

"Well," she paused. "He died of pneumonia."

"Pneumonia, I didn't know you could die from it," he replied.

"Yes, you can; however, Tracey's pneumonia was bought on by AIDS. He was HIV positive."

Mychal cleared his throat and squirmed a bit in the bed.

"Any other questions?" she asked looking Mychal in his eyes.

"Uhm... no," was all he managed to say... Although his mind was racing. Miracle started running her legs up and down his body. Mychal didn't respond.

"What's wrong Mychal? I've apologized several times and told you no more secrets. You never turn me down," she hissed.

"I need to use the bathroom," he said. The guilt and the anxiety of Miracle's words made him feel ill. He was such a hypocrite.

Mychal jumped up and quickly walked into the bathroom. Miracle heard him in the bathroom and it sounded like he was vomiting.

She yelled, "You okay?"

She walked to the bathroom, but the door was locked. How strange. He never locked her out.

What the hell was going on, she wondered.

"I'm fine," he yelled back.

"Why did you lock the door?" she asked.

"Give me a minute. The food at the airport must have been bad," he replied.

Miracle thought it was strange because she ate the same thing and she was feeling fine.

"You want me to get you some ginger ale," she yelled through the door.

"No. I'll be okay. I'm fine, Mir. Really... Just give me a minute."

"Okay," she countered.

Miracle was perplexed. She hadn't seen Mychal vomit since he had the flu, years ago. Her husband had an iron stomach and could eat anything.

This was unusual. The drama of the last couple of weeks weighed heavily on her. Miracle felt a rush of emotions—sadness and tiredness had overcome her body.

She retreated to her bed to wait for Mychal to come out of the bathroom.

Chapter Twenty-Four

Mychal

Mychal looked at himself in the mirror and couldn't believe it, after all of this time, he saw the one person, other than his wife, who gave him one of the best orgasms of his life—dead in a coffin. He had flushed the night out of his head—a long time ago. It felt like the bile was moving back up. Mychal was able to keep it down.

"AIDS," he said to himself. *How? Why?* The thoughts were rambling on in Mychal's head.

He never thought he would have to deal with "that" night ever, again. It had been a secret all this time and he thought he would take it with him to his grave. He was getting paranoid. It had been years since he slept with Tracey, but now he was wondering, if he had AIDS. He was calling the doctor first thing in the morning. It was time for a check-up anyway.

What if he had it?

Mychal was starting to freak out.

He needed to pull it together; beads of sweat drenched his pores. Miracle was waiting and he definitely wasn't ready to discuss what was going on. He wanted to get tested first.

How would his wife take this news? He shook his head. *God, please, no!*

There's a possibility that my life is about to turn upside down for a stupid mistake I made in college.

Why? Why now? Are you kidding me?

As big as this world is my brother-in-law had to marry the one person in the world, who could cause me to lose it all, because of one indiscretion.

What did I do to deserve this? He thought. This was a come-to-Jesus moment for Mychal.

He realized how quickly your life can change and we really have less control than we think. God has a way of getting our attention, when we least expect it. It's funny, how we think we're doing it all—until something happens. Thank God, we can call on Him. He hears our prayers.

Mychal needed to get out of the bathroom before Miracle started banging at the door again. There was no way he was going to make love to his wife tonight. His mind was too cluttered; he couldn't, even if he wanted to.

For the first time in a long time, Mychal Alexander was scared. It didn't happen much, but this right here was enough for a lifetime.

Thank goodness, when he came out of the bathroom, Miracle was asleep. She looked so beautiful and peaceful. His heart ached as he thought of the raft to come. He loved his wife. He never cheated, worked extremely hard, loved his children and did his best. Now, his world was being shaken, like a tree. He just had to remember that his roots were planted in Jesus.

Karma had always told him, "Don't forget who gave it all to you. Keep yourself rooted in His word."

He used to laugh and shake his head at his sister. He believed, but sometimes he was a bit arrogant and failed to realize he wasn't doing it alone—until now.

Mychal was up and ready for work before the hustle and bustle began. He couldn't face Miracle and needed to get out of the house, before the questions from last night started all over again. He looked at his wife and his eyes began to tear up.

Mychal called his doctor's office as soon as they opened. He got lucky. They had an available appointment in an hour. He left his office in a panic.

"Mr. Alexander, we will call you in a couple of days with the results. Do you give us authorization to release your results to anyone else besides you?" the nurse asked.

"No, only me," he advised.

"No problem," she confirmed.

Mychal left the doctor's office and didn't feel like returning to work. He really needed someone to talk to before he lost it.

"Karma," he whispered.

She wouldn't judge. Karma would give him the truth whether he wanted to hear it or not. He called his office and told his assistant that he wasn't returning, but could be reached by phone, if needed. Mychal headed his car towards his sister.

Karma was sleeping. He stood there and looked at his sister for a few minutes. She had lost weight, but her face looked peaceful, as she slept. He really didn't want to wake her, but he needed her right now. It bothered him, a little bit, that he had to bother her with his problems, when she was dealing with her own issues.

That's what he loved about Karma, she would still help others, while she was going through something herself.

Just then, Karma opened her eyes.

"How long have you been standing there?" she asked.

"Just a few minutes," he responded.

He bent over and kissed his sister on her cheek.

"How are you feeling?" he asked.

"I'm doing okay. I have my good days and I have my bad ones, but I'm still here, so I won't complain," she smiled. "How are you doing?" she asked. "You look troubled." Karma had a way of looking into people's soul. It was like she had a connection with your soul and could sense dissension.

"We are talking about you, right now," he said.

"If you weren't in bed, I would beat you. Why didn't you

tell me that you were sick? I would have been here sooner. You need your family, now more than ever. I can't even believe your husband left. Well, let me take it back. I can believe it. He was always weak to me, anyway," he added.

"Mychal, see, that's why I didn't want you to know."

"I'm sorry, sis, but it just burns me up that he would leave when you need him the most. I can't stand weak men. That's all I'm saying."

"Everyone can't handle life, Mychal. He just couldn't deal with it. I would rather he leave, than be here and make it more miserable for me. I wouldn't be able to handle him and this cancer, he didn't want to be with me; so, I prefer he left. I don't need anyone around that doesn't want to be here."

"Is it hard?"

"Hell, yes, but I serve someone who is a heart fixer and a healer. He can take the pain and turn it around. I've been focusing on the glory in His name and no other. One thing, I have learned is man will always let you down, Mychal, that's why you can only put so much faith in them. They want to do right, but sometimes they just can't. Walter is one of those people and I actually feel sorry for him. Shoot, more than I do for myself, because I know what's going to happen to me. I will rest my eyes on my living savior and be forever blessed. I pray for Walter every day, because he's lost; and to me being lost is more painful than this cancer in my body."

"Damn! Girl, you are deep. I don't know how you do it," he said.

"Do what?" she asked.

"Stay so damn positive, when things look so dim."

"It may look dim to others, but honey, I see the light. Don't get it twisted. I have my days, as well. Please, don't make me out to be a saint." She laughed. "By no stretch of the means, am I always positive. Like I said earlier, I have my good and bad days," she smiled.

"Now, back to you. What's going on with you? I know you, Mychal. Wait, how is Joseph?" she asked. "What's going on with him? Miracle, told me she was in Atlanta helping him with an issue."

Mychal let out an expected sigh.

Just the thought of the funeral bought back memories, he wanted so hard to forget.

"What was that about? What happened? Is Miracle alright?"

"Slow down. Can I get a word in?" he asked.

"Sorry," she said.

"Miracle is fine. Everything went as well as expected at a funeral."

"Funeral? Who died?"

"Tracey, Joey's husband."

"What are you saying?"

"You heard me. Josephs' husband died."

"I had no idea," Karma said looking shocked. "I mean, I never met him, but I had no clue he was married to a man."

"Me, either," Mychal smirked.

"How did you not know?" She was really confused. "Didn't you go to the wedding?"

"No." Mychal said turning towards the window.

"Wow!" Karma replied. "I'm sorry to hear that he lost his uhm, uhm husband, I guess. It just sounds weird even saying it," Karma admitted.

"Is that what has you so upset? The fact about Joseph being married to a man. I know it's a serious shocker, but why would it have you so upset. What's really going on, Mychal?"

He knew he could speak frankly with his sister and she wouldn't judge. However, it still makes him feel uneasy to open up about something this embarrassing and so out of his character.

Would she think differently about his manhood, if he made this confession about an act he committed so long ago, as a stupid young man?

It was eating at him like piranhas. He had to release it to help heal his guilt. He figured what the hell.

"I came here because I need to talk to someone before I explode. I don't even know where to begin," he confessed.

He got up and walked over to the window and gazed out for a minute. He walked back, sat down and pulled the chair closer to the bed. He looked Karma in her eyes.

"Sis, what I'm about to tell you, can't leave this room. It's between you and me."

"Okay," she said. She was looking genuinely concerned.

"When I was a junior in college, I had a homosexual encounter with another basketball player from an opposing team that we played."

Karma raised an eyebrow, but didn't speak.

Mychal paused for a moment. "You know I had been pursuing Miracle, since we got to school, but she never wanted to take it to the next level. Well, she finally agreed to go out with me and I was so excited, but I screwed up. She came to my dorm early for our date and she caught me with another girl."

Karma looked confused, but still didn't speak.

"Let me finish," he added seeing the confusion on her face. "The next day, we had a game. Afterwards, there was a party and Miracle was there. Of course, I tried to talk to her and she wanted nothing to do with me. She left the party and I began drinking heavily. I was a mess. There was this guy who came over to me and we started talking. We had a lot in common and I confided in him about Miracle and God knows what else, because I was twisted. Anyway, I started feeling bad, so he helped me to my dorm. One thing led to another and you can figure out the rest without all the details, I'm sure."

He got up again and walked over to the window.

Whew! He had finally said it aloud and it felt good. It was as if a burden had been lifted from his heart.

Karma was still quiet and gave him his time to absorb his renewing. She knew the feeling all too well, when you released pain and your mind and spirit starts to refresh.

Mychal turned around and looked at Karma. He wanted to see her face and see if there was disgust or disappointment. There was neither. She smiled and patted the bed. Karma moved over and allowed her brother to sit next to her.

She hugged him and whispered in his ear, "It's okay."

The flood gates opened and Mychal cried like never before. He released and washed away all of his embarrassment and sequestered pain. Karma held him tight and let him liberate himself.

When Mychal was done crying, Karma wiped his face and kissed his cheek. It was reassurance for Mychal and she hadn't crucified him for his actions. It meant the world to him at the moment.

"Do you feel better?" she asked.

You've been holding it in for far too long, so I know it felt good to finally get it out," she insisted and smiled.

He shook his head. The words didn't want to come out. He was still too emotional.

"Okay, I'm a little confused," she said. "What does it have to do with the funeral? Did experiencing someone dying, so young convict you to open up about this deep secret?" She looked at him intently.

He was slow to speak. "Hold on, I'm getting to it. I just need a minute."

"Take your time," she replied.

"I'm at the funeral and I walk up to the casket, I look down and who do I see, but the guy I had the sexual encounter with all those years ago. I almost died myself. Talking about being shocked and having the wind knocked out of you. I thought I was going to lose it. I held it together, though. Miracle could tell something was wrong, but I down played it and diverted the attention back to Joseph and the matter at hand. It worked only because of what was going on. We got back home and things got a little heated, because she wanted to have sex and I kind of pushed her away."

"Why did you do that? Were you feeling guilty, because of what happened all those years ago?"

"Hell, yeah! But that isn't why I did it," he added.

"Then, what?"

"I also found out that Tracey died of AIDS, well not, AIDS. He died of pneumonia, but he had AIDS."

"No!" Karma exclaimed. "Sorry," she admitted. "Wow, so you mean to tell me of all the darn people in the world, Joseph married the one guy in the world you had sex with."

The sound of those words made Mychal cringe a bit. He

knew he had just said it out loud, but it felt different coming from someone else's mouth and landing on his ears.

"Yes," he replied. "I know, right. I was saying the same damn thing."

"The saying reigns true, 'It's a small world,'" she added.

"AIDS," she said empathetically. "Oh, no, Mychal," She covered her mouth as it all sank in. "Miracle," she softly whispered.

"Yes, Miracle," he said out loud.

"Have you told her?"

"Hell, no." he said aloud.

"Sorry," he said. "No, Karma. I can't. That's why I'm here. I don't know what to do. I'm so confused. Everything in my being is saying tell her, but then the other sensible side of me is saying, 'Are you an idiot? You better keep your mouth shut, fool.' I have so much to lose."

"You have more to lose by keeping secrets and living a lie," Karma gently said. He knew she was right, but those are words. To actually live in it and understand the implications of releasing this information to the one person on earth that trusts him with her whole existence scares the hell out of him.

What if she doesn't forgive him? Even though it happened before they were together. He had withheld some detrimental information from her, not allowing her to make a decision of whether she wanted to marry a man who had been intimate with another man. That's deep. He continued to wonder in that moment. *What would have happened, if he had told her? Would she be his wife, today?*

Only God knows, now.

Hell, would she continue to be his wife, now, once she found out, he thought. *It scared the shit out of him.*

Karma could see the worry on his face.

"Mychal, get out of your own way for a moment," she said. "Let me play devil's advocate for a minute. How would you feel if the shoe was on the other foot? I always ask myself the question when dealing with things like this. Do unto others, as you would have them do unto you. (Luke 6:31 MEV). She quoted. If this was Miracle's story, wouldn't you want to know? Or feel that you had the right to know. It's easy when it's us in the mess to hide the truth; however, if someone else is lying to us or withholding information, we are quick to turn away and not want to forgive them. You should take the 'I' out of this equation and look at the whole picture through her eyes. It's only fair. I know you don't want to hear this, but you came to me and revealed your truth, so now, I must give you what's in my heart. If not, I'm being a hypocrite and it won't sit right in my soul. Furthermore, you can't predict what Miracle is going to do, but I can tell you this, if you don't tell her and she finds out some other way, it will be worse. You can take that check to the bank and cash it. It will clear all day long," she added.

He smirked.

"Corny, but true," she shrugged.

"I just need some time," he said.

"Time," she repeated. "Time is something we don't have a lot of," she laughed.

"Trust me, you don't need time, nor have time to waste. You've had more than enough time. This happened how many years ago," she chuckled. "Honey, I think you've had all the time you need. Stop making excuses and talk to your wife, the mother of your children, the women who you made a vow to and promised to be open and honest to, no matter what, God will handle the rest, once you confess. He has your back. Shoot, he has your back, front, side and every other angle. You must trust in Him with all your heart. He can fix it. I know he can. I don't doubt it for a minute. When you leave and on your way home or wherever you're going, promise me that you will Google and listen to 'I Need You Now' by Smokie Norful and follow it up with 'Closer Walk with Thee' by Fred Hammond and Rueben Studdard. Those two songs, right there, will change your heart. God will minister to you through those lyrics. Promise me."

"I will," he replied.

"Mychal, look there has never been a promise that life would be easy or proceed without spot or wrinkle. All we can do is our best and try to make it through the green lights quickly and safely; we must wash out the spots and iron out the wrinkles. Life is too short for games and tricks. 'Tricks are for kids' and we were kids a long time ago. I'm on a roll," she laughed. "Seriously," she said. "This is not a laughing matter, but we must see a little humor in all things or we will go crazy. I will be praying for you and your family. At this point, it is all I can do. I will never share this information with anyone, unless you ask me to. You have my word on it; however, you must do what is right for yourself, first and foremost, and then, for your family. It's only noble and it's what God expects of you. He has allowed you to carry it this long, but everything eventually comes to the light and truths must be admitted. Now, is your time. I'm done," she said.

He knew everything she said was right.

"Thank you," he said. "I appreciate your opinion and honesty. I know I can always depend on you. You are my soul of righteousness. I'm going to pray on it and listen to the songs you told me about. I want to wait for the results of the test, so I can reveal everything at once," he added.

"Test?" she questioned.

"Yes, I went to the doctor, today and got tested for HIV/AIDS. That's where I'm coming from," he admitted. "I read that the virus can go undetected for like ten years and I know it's been longer than that, but after finding out, I had to get tested just to make sure. We don't need any surprises and I want Miracle to be at ease. You just never know."

"Sure," she said. "I can understand. See, at least you took some action in trying to make it right. I know in my heart, it will be alright. However, God sees fit to fix it. You will be fine. There is nothing like going through a storm with all the wind and rain, but when it's over and you see the rainbow in the sky, you realize God is still in control and it will be alright. The key word here is 'THROUGH.' I didn't say stuck in a storm. That's something totally different. Stuck means no forward movement to be hindered. As long as we keep moving, you're going through. Remember that. And don't wait too long. As they say, 'Study long, Study wrong,' that's the last thing I'm going to say."

"Now, what are you going to do about your situation," he asked. "You've listened to me, but you're going through a storm also," he explained.

Karma laughed, "Yes, I am, but this too shall past. I am just living each day I'm given to the fullest. I'm ready to get out of this hospital and to go home. I already told the doctor, if this last treatment he wants to try is unsuccessful, I want to go home and have hospice care and let the cards fall where they may. I have come to grips with this thing and I know only God knows the end and I'm good with the outcome. I'm banking on a miracle, if not I want to enjoy the time I have left with my children and family; and try my best to be at peace. All of my ducks are in a row, as they say. I'm ready either way," she laughed. "Only time will tell, my brother."

He hugged and kissed his sister on the forehead.

"I'm here for whatever," he replied. "I love you, Karma."

"I love you more, Mychal," she said and winked.

Chapter Twenty-Five

Mychal

The next couple of days were a little tense for Mychal, but he did his best to make it seem normal—whatever that was. He had come back from his morning run and Miracle was still in the bed. He placed his iPod, Fitbit and cell phone on his nightstand by the bed. Mychal walked into the bathroom and turned on the shower. The hot water felt good on his body. He wished the water could wash all his secrets right down the drain, as easily as the dirt. The water pounded his body and he welcomed it. This was eating him alive. He was such a hypocrite—telling Miracle to always be open and honest with him; yet, he was holding back and lying to her, "You're a joke, dude," he muffled.

Miracle was awakened by Mychal's cell phone. It startled her. She looked up and reached for the phone.

"Hello," she said.

"Hello, may I speak with Mr. Alexander, please?"

Miracle heard the shower. He's unavailable, right now. Can I help you with something? This is Mrs. Alexander," she said trying to get the bass out her voice.

"No, Ma'am," the voice said politely.

"Okay," Miracle said. It was a women's voice. Her heart skipped a beat, but she pushed the thought out of her mind, as quickly as it entered. She knew better. Or better; yet, Mychal knew better. The women on the other end of the line must have sensed the hesitation in Miracle's voice.

She quickly added, "I'm sorry, Ma'am, this is his doctor's office and I need to speak with him, personally. I can't discuss this information with anyone other than Mr. Alexander," she explained.

"I'm not anyone," Miracle said a little snooty.

"I understand, Ma'am," the women replied, "but I must uphold the HIPA law or I could get in trouble. I'm not allowed to share the information without approval from your husband."

"Approval from my husband," Miracle pondered.

What the hell was going on, she wondered.

"Okay," she said. "I get it."

"Once again, sorry Ma'am, but I can't afford to get in trouble and lose my job."

"No, I fully understand," Miracle said relaxing a bit.

"Mrs. Alexander, can you, please, have your husband call his doctor's office, as soon as possible?"

"Yes, I will," Miracle responded.

"Thank you, so much," the voice said and then the line was disconnected. Miracle looked at the phone.

What the hell was that all about? She thought. The water shut off.

He didn't tell me he went to the doctor.

She knew that he didn't have any appointments scheduled, because she scheduled all the family doctor's appointments. Mychal walked in the room with the towel wrapped around his waist. Water glistened on his chest. She had to admit this man was still fine as the day they met and his body was just as tight. He went through great measures to remain in shape and she admired that about him.

Her weight went up and down. She had a certain limit and she refused to go over it, if she started gaining weight.

Mychal saw her holding his phone. She was looking a

little confused.

"What's up?" he said.

"Your phone rang and woke me up. I answered it and it was your doctor's office. They want you to call them," she said. "The nurse wouldn't tell me anything. Is there something I should know?" she asked.

Mychal stood frozen.

Oh shit, he was thinking.

His heart started to beat fast. He was so tired of walking on egg shells. He just wanted to tell her the damn truth already. He walked over to the bed and sat down. He grabbed her hand and kissed it. Mir, I have something to tell you and I don't know how you will react."

"You're scaring me," she said. "What is it?"

"Just give me a minute," he said. He got up and walked over to the window and said a quick prayer.

Lord, please, help me make it through this. I need you now. Amen. Mychal walked back to the bed and sat next to Miracle and looked straight in her eyes. His eyes began to tear up, but he held them back.

"Mir, you know, I love you more than life itself and would never do anything to hurt you. I would do just the opposite. Do whatever it takes to protect you."

She tried to answer, but he put his finger to her lips. "Please, just listen. Don't say anything until I'm done, otherwise I won't be able to get it out," he confessed.

She nodded her head, but didn't say anything. Her eyes looked so bewildered and confused. It killed him a bit inside to see her like this, because of him.

Mychal told Miracle the entire story from beginning to end. He didn't leave out one detail.

Miracle was speechless. Tears were streaming down her cheeks. Her marriage was playing before her eyes—their initial meeting, the first time they made love, their first house, all the vacations, the birth of their children, the hot sex, the good times, the bad times and everything else in between.

She envisioned her husband and Tracey having sex and she immediately rushed into the bathroom and released the contents of her stomach. She was crying—uncontrollably.

Mychal walked into the bathroom and his heart had dropped to his feet, when he saw his wife on the floor hugging the toilet bowl. He wanted to reach for her, but was afraid of what her reaction would be to him.

Instead, he walked over and got a warm wash cloth, so she could wipe her face. He handed her the cloth. She just sat there still staring at nothing in particular. He got down on the floor next to her and began wiping her face. Miracle didn't move. Mychal didn't know what to do.

He picked his wife up off the floor and carried her back to the bed. She was in shock.

"Miracle," he said softly. "Please, say something."

He was getting choked up. "Mir, I need for you to say something. Please, yell, scream or cuss, baby. Do or say something," he begged.

She didn't respond.

"Okay," he said. He got up and walked into the bathroom. "I'll give you some time," he whispered.

He closed the bathroom door and slid down to the floor. He cried like he had never cried before. He released all the pain, guilt and shame with each tear. The lies, the hurt, the pain and the joy of being free from the secret he had hid, for so many years. No matter what happened, he could finally let go of the guilt, he was carrying for something he did as a young man. It was liberating.

Now, it was time for him to get up, get himself together and win his wife back. He would stop at nothing to make sure he didn't lose the love of his life.

Chapter Twenty-Six

Patrick

"What's going on, baby?" Patrick asked. "You've been walking around here like the world has ended. I'm not used to seeing you like this."

Patrick waited a moment for Miracle to answer him. When she didn't, he said, "It's a nice morning, Isn't it?"

Patrick was sitting at the kitchen table. She didn't reply to anything he said or even grunt.

Miracle was in the kitchen doing the movements, but she had no clue what she was doing. She felt like her world had ended. She was numb. Miracle knew she couldn't continue to operate like this, because she had people depending on her. She was the glue holding the family together and if she wasn't sticking anymore, the family would fall apart.

It is easier said than done, she thought. *The devil is busy,* she thought *and he doesn't have to use a lie. He knows exactly where to attack and make it for real.*

Miracle's family was his point of attack, but he's a liar. "You can't and won't have my family," she said out loud.

"What did you say?" Patrick asked. He thought Miracle was talking to him.

"Nothing, dad," she replied.

"Thank goodness, you are alive," he joked. "I've been talking to you and this is the first response I get. I thought you were walking dead."

He didn't know it, but that's exactly how she felt inside. Dead! Miracle knew she had to pull it together, before too many questions started to fly from her dad and the children. This was something she and Mychal would have to work out. She absolutely didn't want her children to know any of this story.

"I'm sorry, dad, I just have a lot on my mind, right now. It has been one thing after another, but I will be alright," she smiled.

Patrick hated seeing his daughter like this. He needed her strength right now, even if he didn't want to admit it. He was having a difficult time. It was getting worse every day. Miracle had been so busy with Joseph and the funeral over the past couple of weeks that she didn't realize how quickly his illness was progressing.

Patrick was scared to death. He had never experienced anything like it. This was worse than any war he fought in. He was facing a war within himself and he was losing the battle. It was the hardest part for him. Marines are supposed to be able to attack and destroy—any enemy. But this enemy could not be defeated. It's called life and aging.

"Dad, I'm calling the doctor today to make you an appointment. I didn't forget," she said. "We are going to find out what is going on with you. I know you think nothing is wrong, but something is going on. Don't worry, we will figure out what it is."

Miracle was still wandering around the kitchen aimlessly and wasn't looking at her dad. She heard whimpering. He was weeping. "Oh, dad," Miracle went and pulled him in her arms. "Dad, it's going to be okay. We will get through this together, it will be alright. I will be here every step of the way," she assured him.

Miracle had never seen her father cry. He didn't even shed a tear when his wife died. This startled her. She knew this must be serious. Patrick was like a rock and he never displayed weakness—ever. It was the Marine in him.

"Baby, I'm scared," Patrick confessed. "For the first time in my life, I'm afraid," he mumbled. "I've dealt with the mean streets, fought in a war and faced a lot of crazy things, and I handled it, but this, right here, has me scared to death. When I faced all of those other challenges, there were two key factors making me invincible: one was youth, and the other was your mother. I have lost both and now, I'm just an old man facing this thing without my two greatest factors," he admitted. "When you're young, you think you can conquer the world and with your mother in my corner, I believed I could defeat anything, as well. What scares me the most is I'm losing the memory of it all. My saving grace with getting older and not having your mother was my memories of her, but now that's slowly slipping away, too."

He was sobbing uncontrollably, now.

Miracle's heart melted. This was the first time in her life that her dad let down his guard and showed her any type of weakness. They spoke all the time and had a great relationship, but he never showed this vulnerable side of himself—to Miracle. She was sure, her mother saw it, but not her.

He had been taking care of her, since she was a little girl. Always protecting her, but now the roles were reversing. It was like he was the child and she had to protect him. She would go to hell and back, to do it. Nothing would stop her. Miracle would honor her father, just as he honored his family. He made sure they were all taken care of to the best of his ability, including Joseph. Her dad and Joseph had their issues, but no one else could even think about hurting Joey. He wouldn't have it. He didn't agree with Joey's lifestyle, but it didn't change the fact that he was still his son.

Miracle wiped her dad's face and looked him straight in the eyes.

"Dad, we can beat this. Even, if this means I have to be your memory, then, so be it. Whatever it takes to get through this, we will. Trust me, we will come out on top. Mom's presence will never be gone from our lives." She kissed him on the cheek and smiled.

His eyes looked so sad. "Do you remember when mom got sick and we just knew our lives were going to fall apart, because of her illness? The last thing I remember her saying was 'Jesus doesn't give us a spirit of fear.' Those words ring loudly in my ears, whenever I face any challenge. I must admit, it was chaotic for a while, but we made it.

This isn't any different."

She tried to encourage him. "We can do this," she blatantly stated. "We are built for this with strength and fortitude. We are Jones' dammit. We don't give up easily. You taught me that and it has gotten me through a lot of tough times. The same strength and drive will get us through this hurdle, as well. We can't stop running. We must run and hit it head on."

Miracle was hearing what she was saying in her own head, as well. She was facing some challenges and she needed this advice, as well. People are good at solving other's problems, but they don't deal with their own mess. She was preaching to her own choir.

"Dad, I love you. We got this. Trust me."

His eyes softened a little, but Miracle could tell he was still afraid, but it's understandable.

"I'm going to go call the doctor to make an appointment. Hopefully, we can get in today or tomorrow, at the latest."

Patrick was so grateful for his Miracle. She was always the voice of reason. It was one of her gifts.

"Thank you, baby," Patrick said. "You are so much like your mother. She was really the rock of the family, just as you are with your family. Most women are, even if the man doesn't want to admit it."

"Yeah, you must not be feeling well," Miracle joked. I never thought I would hear you say that in a million years."

She tried to cheer Patrick up. He smiled.

"Well, I said it. I'll never repeat it, but I did say it."

"Dang, I wish I had my voice recorder."

They both laughed.

It was good to see her dad laughing.

Miracle called the doctor's office and they had an appointment available later in the afternoon. Miracle got everyone out of the house in record time.

Patrick was in his room resting. She had a couple of hours before she had to take him to the doctor's office. She tried to work, but her mind wouldn't allow it. She was dealing with so much and it was like a snow ball rolling downhill. It kept getting bigger and bigger. She needed to relax her mind or she was going to explode.

Miracle had a thought and then she laughed to herself. She hadn't done it in years.

"I don't think so," she said. "I've probably lost it," she told herself.

"There's only one way to find out," she said.

Miracle walked out of the house and into the backyard. She opened the shed that was behind the house and flicked on the light. Her stuff was still setup in a corner covered up. There was a mound of dust over the covers. She found a rag and wiped the dust off. Her equipment underneath was fine. The covers had protected the tools. The circular saw, the miter saw and the sander—each with its' own space on the work table.

Miracle got excited just looking at her tools. She used to do woodwork and make all types of furniture and knickknacks. It was her passion and she was good at it. It fell to the wayside, when she began having children. They took priority over her passion.

Her free time had been devoted to her children. She wanted the best for them and she had to make sure they were well-rounded children. It was wonderful, but she lost a piece of herself in doing so. She never complained or regretted it, but she always felt like something was missing in her soul. However, she suppressed it and did what she had to do for her family. The kids were older now and would be leaving home soon and with everything going on in her life, she had to find some outlet or she would go crazy.

I'm kidding myself. She chuckled. *I haven't made anything in years. I don't even know where to begin.*

She had always dreamed of owning her own shop, and selling the items she made with her own two hands.

So, much for that dream, she laughed.

Miracle looked on the shelf to the side of her tools and saw a couple of items on the shelf—items she had started, but never completed. There were pieces for a small footstool, one she had started for her mother. She had planned to give it to her for Christmas, one year. Her mother died, so she never had the opportunity or desire to finish it.

Miracle walked over and took down the pieces. She went over to her work table and sat the pieces down. She turned on her work light. It was like riding a bike. Once you learn, you never forget. She felt like a teenage girl going on her first date. She had energy that she hadn't experienced in years. It was a euphoric high. She couldn't explain it, but she knew it felt good.

She hadn't felt this alive in years. Her problems and worries were in a box locked away, at this moment. She would open it later.

Miracle hadn't realized how much time had passed. She got so engulfed in her work that she lost track of the time. She heard the door of the shed open and looked up. It was Patrick.

"Baby girl, what you doing out here?" he smiled.

"Doing me," she replied. "Finding my happy," she grinned.

"Well, good," Patrick responded. "I hate to stop you, but we have to leave soon, if we're going to make my appointment," he said.

"It's that late already," Miracle shot back. "Wow! I didn't even realize I'd been in here that long," she confessed. "I'll be there in a minute," she said. "Go ahead and get your stuff together. I'm coming,"

"Okay," Patrick smiled and walked out of the shed.

Miracle looked down and was excited at what she saw. It had come together beautifully, if she had to say so herself.

Her mother would have loved it, she thought.

Of course, it wasn't finished, because it needed to be sanded and stained, but the raw beauty was still there. Miracle turned out the lights and walked out of the shed feeling like a new woman. At this very moment, she felt accomplished and empowered.

She knew it wouldn't last long, but for right now, she would accept it and let it fill the corners of her soul. All her problems had been pushed out through her pores by this feeling. She felt like she could face anything.

Thank you, God!

She didn't know what was to come, but she had found her passion—again and she knew she had to find a way to integrate it back into her life, if she wanted to remain sane.

Miracle and Patrick sat in the room waiting for the doctor to come in with his diagnosis. The doctor entered the room and sat on the edge of his desk in front of Miracle and Patrick. At first, Patrick was a little hesitant to tell them all symptoms he was experiencing, but Miracle and the doctor convinced him to be open and honest, because it was the only way they could figure out what was wrong with him.

"Patrick, I'm going be honest with you. We've been friends way too long to sugar coat anything. You have an early onset of Dementia. I would like to schedule you for a CAT Scan and some other testing, so we can pinpoint what type of Dementia it is. There are several forms of this disease. I'm leaning more towards Lewy Body, but I want to be sure. I'm going to have my assistant set up the CAT Scan and the other testing ASAP. I want us to narrow this down, so we can find out the best way to attack it.

Patrick was just starring at the doctor. He knew his memory was getting bad, but he still didn't want to hear this news.

"Is there a cure?" Miracle asked.

"Unfortunately, there is not. Let's not jump ahead. We need to try to figure out what type it is first, and then we can determine the best course of action. Let's get the rest of the testing done and come back together, once we have the results."

Miracle was holding back tears. She didn't want to cry. She knew her dad was having a hard time already, so she held them back.

"Okay," she said. "When do we do the rest of the testing?"

"My assistant is checking the schedule and will be in momentarily with the appointment. I'm sorry, but I'm not giving up hope. I have to see some other patients. Call me with any questions or concerns. I will see you guys back here, once all of the results come in. In the meantime, I suggest you start doing some research on Dementia and Alzheimer's to familiarize yourselves with the diseases, so you can prepare for what's to come. This isn't to scare you, but to inform you. Please, remember each case is different and each person handles this disease differently. Don't get discouraged with your researching. Remain positive and I will do everything in my power to ensure we're doing what we need to do on this end to make sure you all get through this informed and well-equipped. Talk to you soon."

He shook both their hands and left the room.

A few minutes later the assistant came in and said there was an appointment available early next week, if it fit their schedule.

"We can make any day and time you tell us."

"Okay, great," she responded. "I will write it down for you. You all can get yourselves together and come out when you're ready. Stop at my desk and I'll give you the appointment card and referral telling you where you need to go for the test."

"Thank you, so much," Miracle responded.

The assistant walked out of the room and closed the door. Patrick and Miracle just sat in silence for a few minutes.

"Dementia," Patrick finally said. "Geez, this is deep. Never in my life did I ever imagine I would lose my mind. I'm a Marine. We are the best of the best. This seems like a cruel joke. Well, baby girl, I guess the old man won't be as funny and witty as he used to be," he smiled.

"I don't know about that," she added. "You will always have a smart mouth, Dementia and all. It probably will be worse and now, you can lie and say you don't remember saying it."

They both laughed.

They got up holding hands and headed out of the office. Patrick kissed his daughter on the cheek.

They knew it would be okay… if they had each other.

Chapter Twenty-Seven

Miracle

Miracle called Joseph to check in on him. She tried to call him every day, but it had been a couple of days, since her last call. She was dealing with her own drama and didn't want to alarm him with her troubles. Besides she was still debating whether she was going to tell him about Mychal and Tracey. Every time she thought about it, the encounter made her cringe.

Does he need to know? Will it change anything?

At this point, she was more concerned about getting Joseph and their dad on speaking terms. He needed them both.

"Hey, Mir," Joseph voiced.

"Hey, Joey, how are you? You sound good."

"Day-by-day, Mir. I've been trying to stay busy. I picked up a couple of jobs, so it has helped me a lot," he said. "I'm just so blessed to be able to work in my purpose and love what I do. It has helped me make it through. If I didn't love what I do, I would probably be crazy trying to find something to keep my mind off Tracey. I tell you, Mir, every person should try to find their purpose and what makes them happy. The world would be a much better place," he added. "Don't get me wrong, it's still hard because when work is over and I'm home alone, the pain and hurt comes, but I'm taking it one step at a time. Mark has been awesome, too. He tries to occupy my down time, so my mind doesn't focus on the loneliness. I'm grateful to have him here. So, what's going on with you," he asked.

"Well, that is sort of why I'm calling," she said.

"What's up?"

"Dad is sick," she said. "We went to the doctor, today, because he had been acting strange lately and when I was down there with you, Mychal found him outside wandering around talking to himself. The cops showed up and everything. But thank goodness, Mychal could explain what was going on, but he has Dementia, Joey. We go back next week for more tests to find out what type it is, but it's definitely Dementia."

Joseph was quiet.

"Joey, did you hear me?"

"Yes, I heard you," he finally said.

"Joey, you must put this foolishness behind you and make amends with dad. We don't know how long it will be, before he starts to forget all of us. I don't want you all to be mad and fighting, while he is going through this illness. He needs you, Joey. Shoot, I need you. I'm going to need help with him. Family will be so important during this illness. Please, just consider it. If you won't do it for dad, do it for me. I'm begging you."

"Miracle, dad said some very hurtful things to me. Words cut deep, Mir and for them to come from your father, the pain hurts even more."

"I know, Joey. I hear you, but we also must forgive. We don't have to forget, but we must forgive. We aren't without spot or wrinkles ourselves," she reminded him.

"Unfortunately, we can't pick our family, so we have to love them. He's sorry, Joey. I know he is or he wouldn't have come to the funeral. He's changing. I actually saw him cry for the first time, ever," she added. "I was shocked. He wants to make things right with you, but you should meet him half way. Life's too short, Joey. You of all people know it firsthand. We go back to the doctor next week for more tests. It would be awesome if you were here. You could use a break from Atlanta, for a while anyway. Think about it. The kids would love to see you, also. I'm going to text you the information, just in case. I'll leave it up to you. I just want you to remember mommy's words. 'Joey, he's still your father.' Remember that. You only get one and once he closes his eyes, you want no regrets."

His mother had told him that on her death bed.

"Wow, that's cold, Mir. You had to bring mommy into this."

"Whatever it takes," she laughed. "Got to go, see you soon!" She had hung up the phone, before he could say another word. Joseph sat there and looked at the phone.

"That heifer," he said and then smiled.

Epilogue

Karma was packing her things, so she could leave the hospital. She was so excited to be going home. She just wanted to sleep in her own bed.

You really can't get any rest in the hospital, she thought. *They come in your room every hour to pick and prod at you. It will be nice to finally get a good night's rest without anyone waking me up,* she thought and smiled.

Mychal would be there shortly to get her. He was going by to pick up the kids first and then, they were all coming to take her home. She was packing her last bit of stuff when the door opened. She turned around to see the tech, who she had talked to a while back.

"Hello," he said. "I heard you were leaving today. I had to come by and see you before you left. I just wanted to make sure you were okay and still praising our Lord and Savior," he smiled.

"Oh, you know I am," she smiled. "That will never change, no matter what happens to me. If I have breath in my body, I will continue to praise Him."

"Amen," the tech said. "I bought you something," he said.

He handed Karma a book entitled, *Daily Prayers and Praises for Women.* It was a journal also.

"I want you to have this book, so you can start writing down your daily thoughts. My mother had one and I found it in her things after she passed away. It really helped me get through the tragic time. I don't want to offend you, but it will be a great memento for your family, whenever the Lord calls you home. And we pray, it's much further down the road," he smiled.

Karma took the book. "I get it," she said. "I'm not offended. I think it's a beautiful idea and I really appreciate it."

"Well, I'm going to let you finish packing. Take care, Mrs. Wright and may God bless you and your family."

Mychal, Seth, Brandon and Jessica were walking in just as the tech was leaving.

"Who was that?" Mychal asked.

"Yeah, mom, who was that?" her son asked overprotectively.

She smiled. "He's just one of the techs working here. He was saying good bye. He's a nice young man."

"Alright," Seth said. "I'm just checking."

"Boy, get my bags." He grabbed her bags.

"You ready?" Mychal said.

Karma looked around the room one last time.

"Yup, she said. "I'm outta here!"

Patrick and Miracle were walking into the hospital to have his follow-up test. They were almost inside when Miracle heard someone call her name.

She turned around and saw Joey walking towards them. She smiled and waved. She was so excited to see him.

"Thank you, God," she murmured under her breath. She knew Joey would show up. And she knew that using their mother's last words did the trick. Joey reached them. He kissed Miracle on the cheek. She didn't say a word.

"Hello, dad" he said.

"Hello, son," Patrick answered. Joseph wrapped his arm around Miracle and they all walked into the hospital together.

Miracle and Mychal were sitting in the therapist office waiting for them to come in. They were going to see a couple who were both therapist. They counseled couples together and separately. This was their first session. Mychal was fidgeting in his seat. He was very uncomfortable and didn't want to share his truths with these strangers, but he agreed, because he vowed he would do whatever it took to get his life back to the way it used to be—before his secret was revealed.

Karma had suggested that they go to counseling. He had set everything up and suggested to Miracle that they attend. She agreed and he was relieved. They really hadn't talked much, since he had told her the news. It was just the basic conversation to make it through the day and to look normal in front of the children.

Miracle sat still with her eyes closed. She was thinking of her woodworking and what project she wanted to do next. She had to think of it to keep her mind from exploding in this office. She knew if she would have to hear the details of Mychal and another man that it would freak her out—again.

Would she ever see him the same again?

The counselors walked in and introduced themselves.

"Hello Miracle and Mychal," the female said. "I'm Dr. Catherine Nelson." She extended her hand to them. "This is my husband, Dr. Samuel Nelson."

"Nice to meet you both," he said and shook their hands, as well.

"Can I get you all anything to drink?" the female doctor asked?

"No." They both answered at the same time.

"Very well, then let's get started. Who would like to start?" she asked. They both looked at each other.

"I think he should start," Miracle said. "He's the reason why we're here," she said rolling her eyes at Mychal.

"Okay," Dr. C. Nelson said. She looked at Mychal and smiled. "It's on you."

Mychal shifted uneasily in the chair and looked down at

the floor. He sighed and looked up and began telling the intimate details of why they were there.

He prayed this would be the last time and this final reveal would be the one to help him save his marriage.

Miracle just looked straight ahead, as the tears ran down her cheeks. It hurt just as much now, as it did when he first told her.

It would take a MIRACLE for her to get over this pain.

THE END

TO MY READERS

I know you have heard it before, but it's true, so that's why it's repeated. Without readers, there would be no authors. We are driven daily to stare at blank pages pulling out our hair and feeling frustrated for one reason—to give our readers an escape. I pray as you read my stories that each one takes you away from whatever your reality is for the moment.

Words can't express my gratitude and appreciation for your support.

I love hearing from my readers with praise and "literary criticism" (seriously). We writers have thick skin, well, at least I think I do… lol.

Remember… you only get one life, so live on the edge, take risk, be kind, smile more and love hard. God, bless you and thank you for supporting me!

ABOUT THE AUTHOR

Author Georgette Littlejohn's love for words began at an early age. She has always been a creative right brain thinker. She is crafty and is fond of the arts. Her passion is writing and interior design.

Miracle's Destiny is her debut novel. The author engages in all genres and published a children's book entitled, "A GRO-c-ERY STORY."

When the author isn't creating stories about her fictional friends she appreciates traveling, cooking, decorating, crafting and most importantly spending time with family and friends.

She lives outside of Washington, DC with her husband and teenage daughter. The author has an adult son, as well.

CONNECT WITH THE AUTHOR

Author Georgette Littlejohn would love to hear from you. She appreciates her reader's feedback. Without readers, there would be no authors. Please feel free to contact her with your comments, questions or concerns. Thank you in advance for your feedback.

She can be reached at: authorgeorgettelittlejohn@gmail.com

You can also follow her blog at:
www.geelovestowrite.wordpress.com

You can follow Author Georgette Littlejohn on:

Facebook: www.facebook.com/authorgeorgettelittlejohn
Twitter: www.twitter.com/geeloves2write
Instagram: www.instagram.com/geelovestowrite

To purchase A GRO-c-ERY STORY
Visit: www.geelovestowrite.wixsite.com/agrocerystory